"I'll do my best to not disappoint either of you."

That small smile crept onto her lips and he wanted to shout his victory. Her smooth skin beneath his thumb sent electricity down his spine. His body tensed at the sudden flood of desire pumping through his veins.

"I know you won't." She placed her hand over his on her cheek.

Trust. Had he ever known anyone quite like Maggie Brown? From a starry-eyed girl to a sultry teenager to this glorious woman standing before him, Maggie would never cease to amaze him.

He kissed her. He'd only meant to kiss her briefly. He wasn't even sure why. He wanted to, so he did. He could taste the vanilla ice cream. Her lips were incredibly soft beneath his. His only thought was he didn't want to stop kissing her.

Dear Reader,

I grew up in a small town in the Midwest. When I needed a story idea, this time I went back to my roots. Brady Ward, the hero, has a lot to deal with when returning home for the first time in years. His relationships with his brother, Maggie Brown, his daughter and even the town come into question. I wanted to capture the essence of small-town living in *Father by Choice.* I loved spending time with these characters and I hope you will too.

I hope you enjoy it!

Best wishes,

Amanda Berry

FATHER
BY CHOICE

AMANDA BERRY

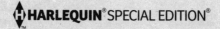
HARLEQUIN® SPECIAL EDITION®

Recycling programs
for this product may
not exist in your area.

ISBN-13: 978-0-373-65744-5

FATHER BY CHOICE

HARLEQUIN®
™ www.Harlequin.com

Printed in U.S.A.

Books by Amanda Berry

Harlequin Special Edition

Father by Choice #2262

Silhouette Special Edition

L.A. Cinderella #2052

Other titles by this author available in ebook format.

AMANDA BERRY

After an exciting life as a CPA, Amanda Berry returned to writing when her husband swept the family off to England to live for a year. Now she's hooked, and since returning to the States spends her writing days concocting spicy contemporary romances while her cats try in vain to pry her hands off the keyboard. Her Marlene Award-winning contemporary romance, *L.A. Cinderella,* was her debut with Harlequin Special Edition. In all her writing, one thing remains the same—love and happily ever after. Amanda lives in the Midwest with her husband and two children. For more about Amanda and her books, please visit www.amanda-berry.com.

To my critique partners,
Jeannie Lin, Shawntelle Madison, Kristi Lea
and Dawn Blankenship, who helped me develop
my idea and create a cohesive story and kept me sane.
I'd be lost without them. To Stephanie Draven,
who helped me make my synopsis the best it could be.
To Missouri Romance Writers, who inspire me and
provide a safe space for those of us with stories to tell.
To my family for putting up with the craziness of a
writer. To my husband for allowing me to live my dream.

Prologue

Eight years earlier

Brady Ward didn't stir as the bed dipped and rose. Maggie's bare feet slapped lightly against the wood floor. The sound of her gathering her scattered clothes from around his childhood room broke the otherwise silent morning. Even the old rooster hadn't woken to greet the day.

The last few stragglers from Luke's graduation party had left minutes before. The sound of engines starting had awakened him from the light sleep. Apparently, it had woken Maggie, as well. His side cooled where her body had been moments before.

Brady remained still so she could slip out of his life as easily as she had slipped into his bed last night. He could almost taste the potential in the air. That this could be more if they wanted it to be. If things were different, they could be more than just one night.

The metal rattle of his doorknob stopped suddenly and he

swore he could feel her gaze on his bare back. As if giving him that final moment to reach out and welcome her back into his bed, give her the promise of something more. But he couldn't give anyone that.

The light floral scent of Maggie drifted over him like a Siren beckoning. Her soft voice lingered in his mind—*I don't normally do this.* Her rich, blond hair had felt like silk in his hands while her hazel eyes had made him feel like the only man in the world.

The door whispered open with a sigh, and she was gone.

Brady rolled and stared up at the ceiling. The graying plaster had cracked, and a daddy longlegs had taken up residence in the corner of his room. He rubbed the dull, familiar ache in his chest.

Last summer had been hard enough. He'd come home from college to help Sam with the farm and tried to keep Luke from getting into too much trouble. Burying the fact that without their mother and father, the three brothers weren't as close a family as they once were.

No use pretending sleep would come. Brady rolled out of bed and pulled on some jeans before plodding down to the only bathroom in the house for a quick, cold shower.

As if he hadn't been away at college for a full year, he fell into the rhythm of chores like he'd always done, because it was expected. Summer break didn't mean he got to laze around the house all day.

By the time the cows were fed and milked, the sheep moved into a new pasture and the pigs slopped, Brady's muscles ached. Being home felt like slipping on a suit that didn't fit right. It had never fit.

Kicking off his muddy boots on the porch, he walked into the kitchen in his socked feet.

"Morning." Sam stood at the stove with a spatula, pushing around brown chunks of what might have been sausage at one point in Mom's cast-iron skillet.

"Morning." Brady started the coffee and hoped there was some cereal or something that didn't need to be cooked—or in Sam's case, burned—for breakfast.

"Glad you could make it out of bed this morning."

Noting the sarcasm, Brady said, "I'm not here to argue with you."

Sam grunted but kept pushing around the darkened meat. "The back forty needs to be plowed. I promised John at least two loads of hay. The barn needs repair and a fresh coat of paint."

"Where's Luke?" Brady tried to divert the conversation from the long litany of chores.

The back of Sam's neck tinged red like it did when Mom had caught him out late. "He went out this morning."

"What did you do?" Reaching into the old white metal cupboards, Brady pulled out their father's favorite coffee mug with #1 Dad emblazoned on the side in red.

"Nothing." Sam cranked the stove off and slammed down the spatula. "Breakfast is ready."

"That *nothing* is definitely something," Brady mumbled as he found a box of Cheerios toward the back of the cupboard. Even stale, it would be more edible.

"Leave it, Brady." Sam's tone left no room for additional conversation. Typical Sam. Which meant that something had happened but Sam was unwilling to confront it. Instead, it would stew inside until he lashed out. Confrontation had never been the Ward family way.

Luke had only been fourteen when Dad died and sixteen when Mom died. If that weren't enough, dealing with Sam for the past two years as his guardian couldn't have been easy. The kid had promised Brady he would straighten out for his senior year. And he had. Luke had graduated with honors and a full-ride scholarship to University of Illinois. He'd managed to escape Tawnee Valley High without a permanent record, an unplanned fatherhood and with all his limbs intact.

With a bowl of cereal and a slightly bent spoon, Brady joined Sam at the table. Sam scarfed down the burned food on his plate. Probably so he wouldn't have to taste it. When he finished, he leaned back in the chair with his cup of coffee and studied Brady.

Undaunted by the appraisal, Brady ate his cereal at his own pace. He might have slowed down slightly to irk his brother. Each bite felt like a lump into his stomach. He should have written a note and left. But he needed to act like the man he wanted to be.

"Maggie Brown is a good kid," Sam said.

Brady knew it had been coming. Ever since Mom got sick, Sam stuck his nose into everyone's business.

"She's not a kid." Even though Brady had seen Maggie around for years, he'd never gotten to know her. Two years behind him in school, she'd just graduated with Luke.

"I suppose not." Sam folded his hands over his stomach. "She seems to have her head on straight. I'm not sure why she slept with you."

The spoon clattered against the bowl. Heat flooded Brady's system, rising until even the tips of his ears were warm. "What of it?"

"She isn't a one-night kind of girl." Sam's fatherly tone had Brady biting his tongue.

Not that it was any of Sam's business, but neither of them had made any promises last night except one night was as far as their relationship would go. There wouldn't be any holding hands in Parson's Park or heading over to Owen, the next town over, to watch a movie and get some dinner. Even if he wanted to, they were at different points in their lives. His plans were taking him far from this place.

"She's the kind of girl you settle down with," Sam added.

Brady shoved away from the table and rose slowly to glare down at Sam's dark hair. "Are you going to arrange a shotgun wedding?"

Sam didn't budge. "I'm thinking you should give the girl a chance. You've only got two more years of school before you come home. She'd make you a good wife and would probably be a better cook than I am."

"If you want a woman's touch around the house, why don't *you* get married?" Brady tried not to think of what Sam was proposing.

"I'm not exactly the catch of the county." Sam's smirk was Brady's undoing. The same damn smirk Sam used to give him when they were kids and Brady had made better grades than Sam had.

"Neither am I." Brady ran his hand through his hair and stared up at the yellowed ceiling tiles. "Don't you see how the people in town treat us? Don't you see the pity? The poor Ward brothers who lost their parents. Hell, in their eyes, you are probably a saint for raising Luke, while I'm the coward that ran away."

"You didn't run away."

"Didn't I?" Brady stared into the blue eyes of his brother that were duplicates of his father's and his. "You don't think I wanted to escape when Mom died? That I needed to escape?"

"And you did. And I didn't stop you." Sam's voice had a slight edge to it. "You went to college, and I stayed here with Luke. I kept the farm going and when you get done with college, you can come home and help out."

"Home?" The word was so foreign to Brady that it tasted bad in his mouth.

"Like Dad always wanted. Like Mom wanted. The three of us together."

The backs of Brady's ears burned. "This isn't home."

Sam's lips tightened. The humor and patience drained from his face. He stood, but the extra inch of height Sam had on Brady wouldn't intimidate him today.

"God, Sam, have you deluded yourself that much?" Brady wouldn't back down. "This can't be home, because home is Mom and Dad. Home was an illusion we had as kids. A safety net to keep us protected. Now? Home is shattered all around us."

"Stop it." The threat behind Sam's words only made Brady push harder. This had been building for too long.

"Luke is a mess. You are a mess. I'm a freaking mess. We don't belong anywhere. You can't keep trying to bind us to this place. We don't belong together."

"Stop." The word was an angry whisper.

"I'm not staying here anymore, Sam." Brady took in a deep breath and the weight released off his shoulders. "I have an internship and scholarship waiting for me. In London."

"England?" Sam staggered backward as if Brady had hit him.

"It's the opportunity of a lifetime. It's what *I* always wanted." Brady changed tactics as some of the anger drained from him. "They don't offer this to just any student, Sam. I'd be a fool not to jump on it. Most people who go end up getting a job overseas. My flight leaves in two days."

"And that's what you want?" Sam straightened to his full height. "To be as far away from here as possible?"

"It's not like after school I'd return to Tawnee Valley, settle down with someone like Maggie Brown and raise a passel of children. The farm is your dream. Not mine."

"What about Luke?"

"Luke?" Brady looked out the window toward the old barn across the drive.

"Who's going to protect Luke? Who's going to watch his back as he tries to become a man?" Sam's voice was tight.

"You were—"

Sam shoved Brady. Caught off guard, Brady almost fell over a chair. The sibling rivalry that had been playing out for years rose to the surface, bringing with it the pent-up rage. But Brady held himself in check, even though he wanted to plant his fist in Sam's face.

"That's right. Me. I'm the one who left college to come home when Mom got sick and Dad died. I'm the one who is stuck on this farm, destined to watch everyone leave our dying hometown. I'm the one who had to step in when Luke made bad decisions. I'm the one who will have to clean up the messes you two leave behind."

"I never asked—"

"Mom did." Sam didn't raise his voice, but he'd struck for Brady's heart.

"But you didn't have to." Brady knew his reply was weak as it left his mouth. The venom from Sam's words seeped through Brady's veins and sapped away his anger.

Their mother meant the world to them. Their parents had tried for years to have children before finally getting pregnant with Sam. Their father had a heart attack when he was fifty-three. That same year their mother found out she had widespread cancer. If the boys could have, they would have taken her place. But none of them could and it was time to get on with their lives.

"I can't keep coming back." Brady took in a deep breath. "Mom's in every square inch of this house. I keep expecting her to come around the corner, to shout from the bedroom for help, to be here. Every time that door squeaks and slams shut I keep hoping to see Dad coming in from work. You have to stay. But I don't have to."

Sam turned and braced his hands against the sink as he stared out the window.

"Please don't ask me to." Brady tried to sound confident, but the words were a shaky whisper.

Sam stared out the window for so long Brady lost track of time. Sam's shoulders sagged from the weight he carried and Brady had helped put it there. Away from Tawnee Valley, Brady could pretend that everything was fine, but here... it hurt to breathe.

Sam finally pushed away from the counter and turned to face him. Brady braced himself to defend his decision. Sam wouldn't understand how hard this was on him. The opportunity was too good to pass up.

"I won't ask you to stay." Sam lifted his gaze to meet Brady's. He didn't raise his voice, but Brady knew he meant every word. "I won't ask you to come home. Not now or ever."

"I wouldn't expect you to." Brady knew this was goodbye. He'd hoped to be leaving on better terms, but knowing Sam, how else could he leave?

"I'll tell Luke." Sam picked up the dishes and took them to the sink.

The conversation was over and so was their relationship. "I'll send what money I can."

The dishes crashed into the sink. Brady winced as the cup he'd given his father cracked.

Sam's words were stilted as he bit out, "I don't need your money."

Brady nodded, but he would send some, anyway. "Bye, Sam."

Chapter One

Eight years later

"Amber! You need to get out to the bus stop now!" Maggie Brown flipped over another paper on the desk. More bills. They just kept piling up.

"I'm going." Amber bounced into the dining room with her backpack strapped tightly to her shoulders, her dark hair swinging from side to side. Her blue eyes were serious, even as she paused next to Maggie's chair for a quick hug.

"You don't have to wait with me." Amber skipped her way out the front door, calling over her shoulder, "I'll be fine by myself."

Maggie rose and followed her. "I like to wait with you."

Amber swung around in a circle, so carefree and full of life. Maggie could barely breathe with the weight on her chest. It had been only a few months since her mother succumbed to cancer. Amber had been their blessing during the hard times.

She'd given Maggie and her mother the chance to focus on life instead of death.

"You all right, Mommy?" Amber had stopped her twirling and walked over to take Maggie's hand. Through the bad times, they had each other.

"Yeah, baby. I'm good."

The squeal of the bus's brakes announced its arrival.

"Time to go." Maggie squeezed Amber's hand and dropped it.

"Love you." Amber flung her arms around Maggie's waist. Before Maggie could return the hug, Amber took off for the school bus.

"Love you," Maggie shouted as the doors folded shut. She wrapped her arms around her waist against the chill of the early autumn breeze that swept the first fallen leaves across the sidewalk. The leaves continued past her neighbor's house. The air felt light and free, but Maggie's insides kept tying themselves into knots.

As the bus pulled away, Maggie noticed a truck across the street in front of the Andersons' house. Not unusual given the teenage kids. It seemed as if a different vehicle was parked there every day. Shrugging off a nagging feeling, she turned to go inside.

Her mom's house needed work. The old Victorian had seen better days, and the wraparound porch needed a fresh coat of paint. But painting would have to wait. Other bills needed to be paid this month.

"Maggie!"

She froze. She'd recognize that voice anywhere.

Spinning around, she saw Sam Ward jogging over from the old white truck. His familiar black hair, blue eyes and strong build marked him as one the Ward brothers. Brady had always seemed more approachable than his stern older brother, though.

Sam stopped in front of her with a grim look on his face. "I'm glad I caught you."

"I was just leaving," she said coldly.

"I saw you at the store with Amber the other day. She's growing up fast." His smile had an edge of worry to it.

Even though everyone in town speculated which Ward brother had done the deed, Maggie had never told anyone except her mom and her best friend.

Luke was always the first guess. They were the same age. It lined up perfectly with their graduation. A few thought it was Sam. Sam didn't talk to her or Amber unless to say a brusque hi if they passed in a store. Not one person in town laid the blame on Brady. He was their golden child, football hero, the most likely to succeed; and he had. He'd gone off to England without a backward glance. She hadn't expected any long goodbyes. And when she'd sent Brady a letter with the fact she was pregnant, Sam had started dropping off money to help. Sam had never said anything, just handed her the envelope or left it with her mother. Brady hadn't even written a note.

As embarrassed as Maggie had been, she'd been grateful for the financial help. But the fact that the Wards, who had lost so much family, didn't want Amber to be a part of their lives left a sour taste in Maggie's mouth.

As far as she knew, Sam hadn't spent any time with Amber. He never stuck around long enough for conversation. Maybe Brady shared the pictures that she sent once a year by mail to the Ward farm like everything else she had to share with Brady. Never any response, but the money always came. Never a note or any request to see his child. Just money, as though that was all Amber needed from her father.

"We go to the same store every week, Sam." She emphasized his name as if he had a few screws loose. "What's this all about? I have to get ready for work."

"I heard about your mom." Sam rubbed the back of his neck. His nervousness was starting to make her worry. What if something had happened to Brady? "I'm real sorry to hear she passed."

"It was the end of a long battle," Maggie said automatically. Even though it had been a different cancer that had taken Mrs. Ward, Maggie knew that in this respect Sam and she had something in common. Her gut clenched momentarily.

They stood there awkwardly for a moment. He looked around as if he wanted to be anywhere but here. The feeling was mutual. "I really need to…" She gestured to the screen door.

He hesitantly stepped on the first step. Apparently, he wasn't going to leave until he'd had his say. "Would you mind if I came in? I need to talk to you."

She stared him down, trying to determine whether she was willing to listen to anything a Ward had to say. But he seemed open and sincere.

She shrugged and opened the screen door. "Is everyone okay?"

"Yeah. Fine as far as I know." Sam followed her into the small living room. Out of habit, she gestured to one of the worn recliners. Her furniture may be worn but it was clean and paid for.

"Would you like something to drink?" Manners won out over the burn of anger. Why now? After eight years of silence, why was Sam here? Was he coming to tell her that Brady was through sending money? She'd have to put in more hours as secretary at the furniture store if that were the case.

"No, thanks." He sat on the edge of the chair, leaned his elbows on his knees and clasped his hands. Then he sat upright and half stood. He gestured to the chair opposite. "This would be easier if you sat."

Her stomach knotted. She moved toward the chair but didn't sit. What would be easier?

"I've done some stupid things in the past, Maggie." Sam seemed to think she was in the mood for confessions.

"I'm sure you have, but I have work to do—"

"Sit down, Maggie Brown." His stern expression had her lowering to the edge of the seat. Obviously remembering where he was, he added, "Please."

"You have a lot of nerve—"

"Yes, I do." Sam ran a shaking hand through his shaggy hair. "You have no idea how much nerve I have."

She crossed her arms over her chest and waited.

"I've done some really stupid things—"

"You said that part already."

He looked up to the ceiling before returning his gaze to her. His eyes softened. "I know Amber is Brady's."

She flushed and started to rise.

"But Brady doesn't."

She fell into the chair as if he'd punched her in the stomach. The air sucked out of the room and she gasped to draw it back in. Blood thundered in her ears. Her thoughts scattered into a million shards. "What are you talking about? I...I told him. He sends money."

His eyes remained sad but determined as Sam reached into his pocket and pulled out some opened envelopes. "I'm sorry, Maggie. I thought I was doing right by my brother. Protecting him. I didn't mean to hurt you or Amber."

She took the envelopes. Each one was a letter she wrote to Brady, including the first one. One for every birthday.

"Brady doesn't know about Amber?" Maggie felt as if the room had turned upside down. With her mother needing constant care after chemotherapy, Maggie had been so startled and scared when she found out she was pregnant that she hadn't known what to do. Brady had vanished overseas somewhere. Taking the cowardly approach, she'd written a letter and sent it to the farm. When Sam dropped off the money, she'd been crushed that Brady didn't want anything to do with Amber, but maybe a little relieved, too.

"I messed up." Sam leaned forward again, his hands clasped before him and his head hung. "I want to make this right."

"Right?" She felt like a mockingbird, but her chest felt hollow and her mind couldn't put her world right side up. All these years, she'd been angry with Brady and he hadn't even known.

All those missed birthdays. The long nights awake with Amber when she'd been sick. Brady had missed everything from Amber's birth to kissing her scrapes and bruises better to holding her when she cried at her grandma's funeral.

A rush of heat went to her cheeks. She could have tried harder to reach out. Even searched for Brady on the internet. But she'd been too afraid of further rejection to reach out through any means but the letters.

"I got you a plane ticket for this weekend and talked with Penny about watching Amber. I didn't open your last letter. You should give it to him in person." He held out the sealed envelope.

She looked at him as if he was the Mad Hatter. "What are you talking about? You walk into my house to tell me you've lied to me and Brady for eight years. Do you know how hard it is to raise a child alone? How hard it is to care for your mother and your daughter when both are sick?"

Maggie jumped up and paced away. This was Sam's fault, not hers. Her mind raced to keep up with her emotions. "You had no right."

"You're right." Sam didn't move from his spot. His face was grim.

"Why?" Her shoulders shook with the anger bubbling

within, but tears pressed against her eyes. A million what-ifs weighed heavy on her soul. Would she have had to do it on her own? Would Brady have held her when her world fell apart? Would he have been the strong one when she felt small and overwhelmed? Would he have grown to resent her for keeping him from his dreams? Or would he have rejected her like his brother had made her think? "Why would you do something like that? How could you treat your brother that way? What did *I* ever do to *you?*"

Sam rose and set the letter and another envelope on the table. He took a heavy breath and blew it out. "I didn't think about you. I had my reasons. It's time to fix this. Go to New York and let Brady know."

"New York?"

"Luke told me Brady transferred to the New York office of Matin Enterprises a month ago. I figured if Brady was this close again, it was time he knew."

"Why don't you tell him?" She shoved the envelopes toward him.

His lips drew into a thin line. For a moment, it seemed as if he wouldn't say anything. But something inside him broke. She recognized defeat because she'd felt it far too frequently herself. She refused to feel any sympathy for Sam, though.

"Because Brady won't talk to me." His words came out stilted and harsh. "He hasn't spoken to me in eight years. The only reason I know anything about his life is through Luke, and he barely speaks to me, either. This is the only way to clean up this mess."

She stared at the plane tickets that had fallen out of the envelope. "I can't go to New York and leave Amber at the drop of a hat. I have a job. I need to work." Her gaze fell on the stack of bills. "I have obligations."

"I'll take care of it." Sam stopped by the front door.

"What? Like you took care of this?" She held the old letters crumpled in her tight grip. Her stomach clenched. Heat flushed through her. This couldn't be happening. Brady had to know. How could he not?

"Damn you, Sam Ward." She made sure all the anger and frustration she felt were directed solely at him.

"I can't change the past, Maggie."

She refused to see the pain in his eyes.

"All I can do is try to fix the future. Brady needs to know about Amber."

Chapter Two

"This project will bring in twenty percent more revenue," Brady said as a trickle of sweat ran along his spine. Senior management filled the boardroom, and he had their undivided attention.

"The project appears to be sound," Kyle Bradford, the CEO of Matin Enterprises, said. In his mid-fifties, Kyle seemed more a friend than Brady's boss. The past month he'd treated Brady to a few football games and a couple of dinners out to discuss where Kyle felt the company needed to go in the future.

Jules cleared her throat and stood, showing off her dark red suit as it hugged her killer curves, though they were nothing compared to the sharpness of her mind. "We put together this project to show exactly what Matin Enterprises can be in the future."

Brady and Jules had put in long hours and weeks of planning to get this project ready for this presentation. Before he'd made the move to New York, Brady had started with the concept and played with the numbers. Now was his chance, and he had known Jules was the right person to help with the project.

"I agree, Kyle." Dave Peterson stood at the far end of the conference table. "However, as a higher-level manager, I would like to help oversee it. That is, unless Brady—" he paused and winked at Jules "—or Jules objects."

Jules had told Brady that Peterson had been asking her out since she started at Matin. Even though she always turned him down, it didn't seem to make a difference. His condescending attitude toward her made Brady want to punch the smug man. The fact that no one else in the boardroom seemed aware of the issue made him more frustrated.

Peterson raised his eyebrow, daring him to make a scene in front of the corporate heads.

"Of course Peterson would be a great asset to have on our team." That way, Brady could keep an eye out for the dagger Peterson would stick in his back.

"Wonderful. Keep us updated as the project moves forward." Kyle stood. The rest of the men and women took it as their cue that the meeting was over.

Brady collected his papers and disconnected his laptop from the projector. Three months of planning had hinged on a one-minute decision.

"Nicely done, Brady." Jules gathered the remainder of their presentation materials. She kept busy as Peterson approached.

Brady shut his laptop and met Peterson's brown eyes. Peterson was only a few years older than Brady, but the man had let himself go over the years. His shirt buttons strained over his stomach, and his receding hairline was a mixture of black and gray.

"Great presentation, you two." Peterson's eyes strayed over Jules's figure. "I couldn't have done better myself."

"Thank you." Brady stopped from adding *because you*

couldn't have. It was well-known among the staff and lower management that Peterson made his way up the ladder on other people's backs, taking credit for their work.

"I expect to be added to all correspondence from now on." Peterson shifted his body closer to Jules. "And included in any meetings you two might have, Jules."

Brady fought the urge to jerk the guy away from her. "Sure, Peterson."

Jules lifted frosty green eyes to Peterson. "We'll make sure you are included in all meetings, but the decisions come from us."

"As long as you're there, I'll be there." Peterson grinned and left the room.

Brady and Jules were both out for the same thing— recognition for the work they did. Their initial attraction had ended with a fizzle after a week. Both of them were driven to succeed and compatible in a lot of ways, but love wasn't in his five-year plan. Jules agreed with him that love was something you sought when your career was firmly in place. Right now, it would get in the way.

"I'll do my best to intervene with Peterson," Brady said, knowing he could do nothing unless Jules wanted to file a harassment report.

She lifted her gaze to his and smiled. "I can hold my own with guys like Peterson. I've been doing it my whole career."

Brady nodded and held the door open for her as she swept by. If he let down his guard for a moment, Peterson would take over his project and get the boost in his career that was meant to be Brady's and Jules's.

An email notification pinged on his phone. He clicked over to it. His blood pressure started to rise as he read the email Peterson had sent out to all the employees working on the project. He'd worded the email perfectly. It implied the project was his baby and that he was *letting* Brady and Jules work it.

Brady would need to keep close tabs on this project if he wanted to keep Peterson from taking over.

"This is ridiculous." Maggie pulled the jeans out of the suitcase and folded them before returning them to the dresser drawer. It had taken every ounce of will Maggie had not to drive out to Sam's farm and cram the tickets down his throat.

"What's ridiculous is how long it is taking to pack a simple suitcase." Penny rested against the headboard with her coppery hair pulled in a knot. Her brown eyes sparkled as she held up a lacy nightgown. "You should take this."

Maggie snatched the nightgown from her best friend's hands and stuffed it into the bottom of her nightgown drawer. She sank on the edge of the bed and put her hands over her face.

"What am I doing?"

"I've been wondering that for the past half hour. Are you packing to go to New York or just testing out your suitcase? I'm fairly certain it can hold more than the blouse you left in it." Penny leaned forward to consider the insides of the suitcase.

"How can I walk up to Brady Ward and tell him, 'Hey, you have a seven-year-old you know nothing about. By the way, it totally wasn't my fault.'" The lump in the pit of her stomach said otherwise, though.

"It *wasn't* your fault." Penny patted her back. "Now pack up and enjoy life a little."

"I should have tried harder."

"To pack. I agree. This is no way to pack to confront the one-night stand you had a baby with." Penny shifted off the bed and started opening drawers. "Not to mention the biggest crush you ever had."

"That's it, Penny. It isn't about me. It's the fact that we weren't anything more than bed buddies for a night."

Penny stopped with a red sweater dangling in her hand and quirked an eyebrow at Maggie. "Bed buddies?"

"Whatever." Maggie took a deep breath. "Shouldn't I call him or email him? Like I should have done in the first place?"

With an armful of clothes, Penny made her way over to the suitcase. "Bygones."

"What if he's too busy to see me? Shouldn't I at least call and schedule an appointment?" Maggie pulled the lacy night-gown out of the suitcase again and tightened her grip when Penny reached for it.

"Okay. I get it." Penny sat next to her on the bed and took Maggie's hand in hers. All playfulness put aside for a moment. "What are you really worried about?"

Maggie's eyes filled with unshed tears. "What if he doesn't want her?"

Eight years ago, her mother had held her tight while she cried over the fact that Brady didn't want anything to do with their baby. Part of Maggie had dreamed that he'd show up on her porch and sweep her off her feet. They'd shared something special that night and relationships had been started under worse circumstances than an unplanned pregnancy.

"Why wouldn't he want her?" Penny squeezed Maggie's hand.

Maggie took a deep breath in. "If he's a self-involved nut job."

Penny smiled. "Then we wouldn't want him around our girl, anyway. Now about this nightgown…"

"No way. Grab my sweats."

"You afraid you'll be tempted to show him your pretty nightgown?" Penny laughed, but Maggie had no idea what to expect when she saw Brady. Would she feel anything? Would her old crush rear its head? Or would she resent him for not being there?

"There won't be anything to worry about. I'll be in a hotel.

By myself." Maggie stood and took charge of the packing. "I should call first, though."

"What could you possibly say on the phone?" Penny tried to mimic Maggie's voice. "I'm planning on being in New York this weekend and ran into Sam. Even though you apparently haven't spoken to him in years, he told me your phone and address so that we could hook up. You don't have time because you are a busy man? That's fine. I'll tell you some other time that you have a daughter."

"I get it." Maggie held up her hands in defeat. She hadn't been able to figure out a better plan for the past few days. "I guess this is the way it will have to be."

Penny grinned and held up a different lacy nightie.

"I'm not going for me. I'm going for Amber." Maggie pointed to the drawer until Penny returned the nightie to its proper place.

"Yes, ma'am." Penny saluted with two fingers. "I guess I don't need to run to the drugstore and get some condoms?"

"No!" Maggie blushed as a little remembered heat flushed her body. "I don't need a man. I've done fine on my own for years now."

Penny muttered, "It isn't about need."

"Where are you going, Mommy?" Amber hugged her brown bear close to her small body. Her hair spread on the pillow, making her look like a dark-haired angel.

Maggie drew the covers to Amber's chin. "I'm going to New York for a few days. Penny is staying with you."

"I like Penny. She orders pizza for dinner." Amber smiled. Her front tooth had come out a few days ago, prompting a visit from the tooth fairy. Another thing Brady had missed out on. If he even wanted to be part of their lives. She tried not to dwell on it, but she had to be prepared for him to reject her like she thought he'd already done. What would he want with a small-town family when he had New York?

"Are you going to see the Statue of Liberty?" Amber asked with awe in her voice.

Maggie smiled. "Maybe."

"Will you bring me something?"

"Definitely." She tickled Amber until she laughed. Maggie had her own ideas of what she wanted to bring home for her, but she wouldn't dare to get Amber's hopes up. It was bad enough that Maggie was thinking hopefully. She'd been kicked enough to only have doubt left, but apparently, a little spark of hope had survived.

"Go to sleep. Penny promised she'd get doughnuts." Maggie dropped a kiss on her daughter's cheek.

Amber linked her small arms around Maggie's neck and pulled her down to the bed. "I'll miss you."

"I'll miss you more, baby." Maggie hugged her as best she could with all the bedding and stuffed animals in the way. She stood and walked over to the light switch. "Good night."

"Night." Amber squeezed her eyes shut like she always did at bedtime with her hands clasped together. What she prayed for, she never said aloud. Maybe Maggie, maybe her father.

Amber knew her daddy lived far away. But Maggie couldn't bear to break Amber's heart by telling her that her father didn't want to be part of their family. Now she was glad she hadn't.

A whole week hadn't been long enough to figure out what to do or say. She'd never imagined Brady didn't know. Over the years, she'd come to terms with the fact that he didn't want her or Amber. Okay, maybe she was upset with him not wanting to be a father, but Maggie didn't need him to want her.

That knot twisted a little tighter in her stomach.

How was she going to tell Brady about their child?

Chapter Three

"This is stupid," Maggie muttered as she stood in front of Brady's apartment building. She should have called. Sam had said she could catch Brady in the morning when he left for work.

The cold day seeped through her jeans and she hugged her blue sweater closer. Her ponytail whipped around into her face again. Just a few more moments then she'd go in and ask for him. Just a few...

Brady lived in a luxury apartment building off Central Park. Housing wasn't cheap in New York, but his building seemed to be the cream of the crop. On the taxi ride over, Central Park had emerged among the buildings. The trees gave an illusion of open spaces, but the massive buildings dwarfed the park, holding it captive. Metal-and-glass structures on concrete. She'd never felt more lost or frightened.

Too many people shoved into one space. Even now, people walked or jogged past her. There didn't seem to be a spare area anywhere in the city to step aside and take a deep breath.

Her heart raced and she could barely breathe with the hustle and bustle.

She didn't understand how Brady could live here when he'd grown up with the open spaces in Tawnee Valley. Where you didn't have to clutch your purse to your side and fear the stranger walking toward you.

She moved closer to the door. Maybe she should return to the hotel and call him. A jogger in hot-pink short shorts weaving between the business people in their gray-and-black suits caught her attention. She followed the woman with her gaze, wondering if she could ever feel that comfortable here, surrounded by strangers.

"Maggie?" Brady's baritone voice rushed over her like a warm waterfall.

Her breath caught in her throat as she turned to find Brady staring at her from a few feet away by the apartment building door. The sun chose that moment to come out from under the clouds, lighting his handsome face as he came toward her. His dark hair was cut more conservatively now, and crinkles formed in the corners of his blue eyes. He was even more handsome than she remembered.

Maggie returned his smile but couldn't form any words. Up close, she could see the similarities between him and Amber. And those eyes, they caused her heart to stutter as he focused solely on her.

Brady had a huge grin on his face. "Maggie Brown! What are you doing here?"

"I came to see you," she pushed out through her numb lips. "I mean, I'm visiting New York and…"

What else could she say? And how was she supposed to think when he looked at her like that? As if he knew her inside and out. It had been a long time since she'd been in his arms, but her body tingled with memories. Should she hug him?

"God, it's good to see you." His genuine smile didn't

change, but his voice sounded different from high school, more sophisticated, colder. "Are you living nearby?"

"No, I'm still in Tawnee Valley." She didn't want to blurt it out, but how was she supposed to ease him into knowing he had a seven-year-old daughter? Even though she'd known Brady since they were kids, they hadn't been close friends, and right now he felt like a stranger. "I need to talk to you about something."

Brady's eyebrows drew together in concern, and he reached out his hand to grip her elbow. "Is everything all right? Is Sam…?"

Shocked at the intense surge of giddiness flowing through her at his touch, Maggie shook her head. No stranger had ever made her feel like that. "Everything's fine."

She wanted to drop her eyes, but his eyes held her entranced. It was on the tip of her tongue to tell him about Amber, but she couldn't make her mouth form the right words.

With his pressed suit, he could have stepped off the cover of *GQ*. The Brady she knew had been headed for big things, but she didn't know this man in front of her. To be honest, she hadn't known Brady even back then. Not truly, just the facade he put on for the town. A facade he let drop during their night together.

"I wish I had more time right now, but I have to get to work. There's an early morning meeting." He pulled out his BlackBerry and checked the screen for a moment.

The cold wind swept through her when he backed away slightly. A reminder that they had shared only one night together. It had been a great night, but it wasn't as if they'd had a meaningful relationship.

Now wasn't the time to tell him about Amber. A little of the weight lifted off her stomach. She couldn't tell him when there were people surging down the sidewalk like salmon around them. When he glanced at her, she shivered and nodded. "Maybe later?"

"How long are you in town?" He gave her the same expression Amber got when she wanted to reassure Maggie. It was unnerving. How could Amber have his expressions when she'd never met him? "I'm not trying to brush you off. Honestly."

He tapped on his phone again.

"I didn't think you were blowing me off." What if this was her only chance? *You have a daughter. I got pregnant. Surprise, you're a daddy!* Maggie swallowed hard.

"Good." He barely looked at her. "How about one? For lunch? Unless you have other plans."

"Sounds great." She forced a smile. *By the way, you have a daughter.*

His return smile stole her breath and emptied her mind. "Where are you staying? I'll pick you up."

She rattled off the address of the hotel. She should tell him now. Get it over with. That way it wouldn't sit in the knot that was her stomach until later. But how? His attention was apparently already at his meeting. She tightened her smile as he glanced at his watch. Who had Brady Ward become?

"I have to run. I'll see you at one." He backed away from her. "I'm glad you came."

By the time they were sitting in the restaurant, Maggie was drawn tighter than a bow. Brady couldn't imagine what had her uptight. The Maggie he'd known had been spontaneous and friendly.

Of course, high school had been years before. But he remembered the adoring look in her hazel eyes when she'd been a sophomore and he'd been a senior. He hadn't taken advantage of her crush then, but two years later at Luke's graduation party, that night he couldn't resist. She'd been stunning and forward and one hell of a kisser.

Eight years hadn't faded her beauty at all. Her honey-blond hair framed her face in a no-nonsense style. She had developed some curves since high school. Her soft blue sweater didn't reveal much, but her jeans clung low to her hips and she filled them out nicely. She didn't try to flaunt her assets the way Jules did. She was just Maggie. She put off a natural vibe that was unlike any woman he knew, and it did something to his senses that he couldn't begin to describe.

"What brings you to New York?" Brady set his BlackBerry on the table, trying to ignore the constant barrage of emails. Now that financing had begun, he had to put everything into motion, which was always the hardest phase and required a lot of finesse. It didn't help that Peterson circled every conversation like a shark waiting for blood.

Maggie lifted her gaze to his. He lost track of what he'd asked as he sank into her rich hazel eyes. Warmth. That's what she offered, with no expectation of anything in return. The type of women he usually went for were like Jules. Sophisticated, driven, focused…temporary.

Her gaze dropped to the tablecloth, then to her hands folded neatly in her lap. "Do you remember Luke's party?"

His phone buzzed insistently against the white tablecloth. He smiled apologetically and fought the urge to curse. The number was the contractor for the new facility. Another fire to put out.

"If you need to…" Maggie said.

"I'm sorry. I need to take this." He stood and stepped outside the restaurant to talk to the contractor about the change orders that had been processed that morning. After a hurried five minutes, they'd agreed on the main changes. When Brady hung up, he quickly scrolled through his in-box to try to avoid more interruptions before heading inside.

She was already picking at her salad when he sat across from her. She looked at him expectantly. He wished for a moment that he could put the rest of the world on hold to catch up with Maggie, but he had obligations. He hoped she'd understand that.

"It was important. I swear it won't happen again." He drew the napkin across his lap. "I'm sorry. What were we talking about?"

"Luke's party?" Her cheeks flushed.

His gut tightened as he recalled that night—her sweet smile and soft kisses. He waited until she looked at him before saying, "I remember."

Her lips parted slightly before she shook herself. She inhaled before taking a bite. Whatever she was working herself up to must be major. The Maggie he remembered had been bold that night. Unrelenting, untamed, unashamed.

"It was the last time I was in Tawnee Valley before I left for London," he said, trying to ease her into whatever she needed to say.

She set down her fork. "I don't know how to even begin to explain—"

His phone buzzed. Brady didn't want to answer it. Something had Maggie tied up in knots. He glanced at the screen. An email notification from Peterson, and Jules was calling. "Dammit. I'm truly sorry. I have to get this one."

He didn't know if she looked relieved or upset as he picked up the call and walked outside. When he returned ten minutes later, their lunch was on the table, but the work situation had been resolved…for now.

"Perfect timing." He tried to lighten the mood.

"You're a busy man." Maggie's statement was soft and nonaccusatory, but it was also a little sad.

"I'm in the beginning stages of a major project. New office. New position. New phone." He held up the phone and then dropped it into his suit's inner pocket. "No more interruptions. How have you been?"

She froze with a bite halfway to her mouth. A little war raged in her eyes until she sighed and put the fork down. "I've been better."

"Is every—"

"Things haven't been all sunshine and daisies the past eight years, but we've gotten through."

His mind stuck on the word *we*. He didn't even know if Maggie was married. His gut tightened. She wasn't wearing a ring, but that didn't mean anything. A memory of Maggie being the kind of girl you married hovered in the back of his mind. Not that it would bother him if she were. He choked a little on the word. "We?"

With her gaze firmly on his, she said, "After Luke's graduation, I found out I was pregnant."

The blood flowed heavy in Brady's ears and the air left the room. "Pregnant? But we—"

"Used protection. Yeah, that was my first thought, too, as I was holding five positive pregnancy tests."

"Why didn't you tell me?" Brady asked quietly, too numb to be angry. A child? How could he have not known? He'd lost track of a lot of people, but someone could have reached out. It'd been eight years. Why keep the child a secret?

She bit her lip. "I wrote you a letter. It was childish. I should have called, but I was scared. We weren't anything more than one night to each other."

"I would have wanted to know that you were pregnant. I don't shirk my responsibilities." He automatically defended himself, but then her words sunk in. Brady's fork hit the plate. "I never got the letter."

"I know."

His brows drew together. "Then why didn't you try to reach me?"

Maggie's cheeks brightened and her eyes flashed. "I didn't know then. Shortly after I sent the letter, I started receiving money. I figured you wanted nothing more to do with me or Amber."

A headache started behind his eyes. "Money? I never sent—"

"A week ago, Sam stopped by. He'd been the one receiving my letters and sending me the money."

"Sam?" Brady felt as if his world was crumbling in on itself. Eight years of lies. He'd been across an ocean, but never out of reach. Brady had sent Sam money for the farm and always included his address and a way to reach him in an emergency. His older brother had always been controlling but this went beyond that. His thoughts stumbled. "Wait. Amber?"

"Our daughter." Maggie pulled a photo out of her purse.

Brady was afraid to take it, afraid to touch it, afraid of making this real. She set the photo in front of him.

"Amber is seven. She's in second grade with Mrs. Mason. She plays softball and takes gymnastics. She's a good kid."

Brady glanced at the photo, meaning to take a peek. But his gaze settled on a face so familiar, it broke his heart.

"She looks like my mom." Brady's hand trembled as he lifted the photo. Tears choked in his throat. It had been ten years since Mom died. When she became sick, it had changed their household. After she died, it had been the three of them. Angry, confused teenagers hell-bent on going their own way. Now his mother had a grandchild she'd never be able to spoil. Finally, a girl.

Maggie gave him a wary half smile. "She looks like you. Every time I see her, I see a little of you."

He had a daughter. His phone clattered in his pocket, insistent for his attention.

He ignored it, trying to grab on to one of the emotions flying around in his head. Anger at not being told, frustration that he couldn't ignore work for even an hour to discuss this with Maggie, confusion over the still-vibrant connection he felt for Maggie and uncertainty on how to process all this.

He had a daughter.

Maggie sat across from him with her usually emotion-filled face as serene as the pond in the back field of the Ward farm. He had a daughter with this woman that he barely knew. A daughter who didn't know her father.

The bubble of a grin threatening to expand on his face burst as his phone once again vibrated violently. Taking it from his pocket, he glanced at the screen.

"Damn." Setting down his daughter's picture, he scrolled through the three new emails. One from Peterson and two from the production leads in response to Peterson's email. "Give me a minute."

He didn't look up as Maggie shifted slightly in her chair. Her outgoing breath was a little harsher than normal. He read Peterson's email and held back the vulgar word that came to mind. Peterson was taking over his project and trying to write his name in Brady's blood all over it.

He couldn't regain his focus as Sam and Amber floated through his mind, each vying for his attention. One with anger and the other with curiosity. And then there was Maggie. He connected with her hazel eyes, and he stopped to take a breath. His chest tightened. "I'm a complete ass. Here I am trying to multitask while you've been doing that for the past eight years. Seven years old?"

Maggie nodded. Seven birthdays. What would his parents think about him not knowing about his child growing up in Tawnee Valley without him? How could he not know? Anything he said or did would feel inadequate for the time he'd missed.

He put down the phone without finishing his response and reached out and took her hand in his. "I wish I'd known. I wish I could have been there for you and Amber. To have to do that all on your own…"

Maggie flushed and dropped her gaze. "My mom was there for us when she had good days."

"Good days?" Brady couldn't remember much about Mrs. Grace Brown, but she'd always been nice to all the kids at the town picnics.

Maggie looked back at Brady. "Mom had breast cancer. She underwent treatment while I was pregnant and we had a few good years before…"

With the revived memories of his own mother still battering his heart, Brady lifted a napkin to the tear that trailed down her cheek. "I'm sorry to hear about your mother."

They both froze at his action. Maggie shifted back and he pulled away quickly, looking at his hand as if it were the hand's fault. He'd stepped over a line. They hadn't ever been emotionally involved.

"She fought it to the end." Maggie's smile was distant, as if she caught a glimpse of some memory that strengthened her. Ten years ago he'd been devastated by his parents' absence from his life. He couldn't even stand to be in the community he'd grown up in.

He had no idea how he would have reacted at twenty to Maggie's pregnancy. He glanced at the posed, smiling face with a few scattered freckles across her nose. Amber. It felt as if a fist squeezed his heart. Had his daughter ever needed him? He winced at the thought of not being there for her.

"I want to see her." The words burst out of Brady before he could stop himself.

Maggie's mouth dropped open.

"I want to be part of her life." A sense of rightness went through him. It's what his parents would have wanted. It's what he wanted. "If you'll let me."

Chapter Four

Maggie's heart raced, but she drew in a deep breath to steady herself. Just because Brady wanted to get to know Amber didn't mean he wanted anything more to do with Maggie. Nothing had to change.

"I'd like that." She tried to smile, but it faltered on her face. "I mean, Amber would love that. It's been hard telling her about you when I thought you didn't want any part of our lives."

Brady's blue eyes narrowed. "I'll never forgive Sam for doing that to you."

"No," Maggie rushed out. Her cheeks warmed. How much of it had been her fault for not trying harder? "I'm not saying what he did was right—"

"It was damn conceited." Brady leaned back in his chair. "He always thinks he knows what's best."

Maggie didn't argue. Brady had been twenty when Sam had made the decision for him. Eight years had added a roughness to Brady's boyish face. If anything, he was more handsome now than when she'd mooned over him in high school. His dark suit and blue tie lying against the soft-gray pressed shirt made him feel less approachable than when he'd been on top of the high school food chain dressed in denim and a worn T-shirt.

His face softened. "I'd do anything to take back those years and give Amber the father she deserved and you the support you needed."

His words irritated her. "We got by fine on our own."

He smiled. "Always the fierce one, Maggie."

The intimacy of the statement hit her below the belt and reminded her why she'd slept with him in the first place. If she hadn't thought he was patronizing her, she might have even liked him saying that. She cleared her throat and lifted her fork to toy with her rapidly cooling food.

He reached for his BlackBerry again and started pressing buttons. "I might be able to get away for a day or two…"

His lips tightened as he glared at the small screen. Whatever was on the screen wasn't making him happy.

"The project I'm working on is a multimillion-dollar deal. But I should be able to get away in a month, maybe a Sunday."

"A month?" The food sank like a lump in her stomach.

"If everything goes according to plan. I should be able to make it out and back in a day."

"It might take longer?" Maggie crossed her arms over her chest. "Amber has waited seven years for a father I didn't think wanted her. What am I supposed to tell her? Your father is a busy man and when he finds time, he fully intends to come meet you for the first time? Am I supposed to string her along with promises of her father indefinitely?"

"Amber should come first. You're right—" Brady met her gaze "—but my career is hanging on this project. Can I fly her and you out here?"

"She has school. No one can cover for you for a few days? You don't have vacation time?"

"Of course I have vacation time. I have a few months' worth of vacation time saved, but—"

"But you aren't willing to take them." She stood and clasped her shaking hands together. "I don't have vacation time, but I came here on my weekend off to tell you as soon as I found out you didn't know."

Brady glanced around them. Some of the nearby diners had stopped talking and stared at them with unabashed interest.

"Will you please sit?" Brady asked softly.

She wanted to leave and forget she had ever come to New York, but she had a duty to Amber. For the past seven years, she'd been the one that Amber turned to, the one she relied on. But every now and then, Amber asked about her father. Maggie wasn't willing to disappoint her daughter because her father was turning out to be an ass. She dropped in the seat and crossed her arms.

"I can't tell Amber that her father *might* be able to make it to Tawnee Valley to see her sometime this year. She's seven. She's never met her dad and doesn't know her uncles. Her grandmother died a few months ago. I'm all she has left."

Brady laid his hand on the table. The surrounding diners went back to their food, but they seemed to lean a little closer in the direction of Maggie and Brady's table.

"I'm not trying to blow you off, Maggie." He ran a hand through his hair and looked up to the ceiling before returning to face her. She had a feeling he said that to every woman in his life. "I want to see Amber. The project I've taken on is important—"

"And we're not." Maggie didn't like the hurt in her voice, but she'd worked hard to be everything to Amber. Now someone else had a chance to be part of Amber's life. This man that Maggie had always found fascinating. He'd been her hero in high school, and it was hard not to be disappointed in the man he'd become. She took in a deep breath and closed her eyes briefly, trying to think rationally. "I know that this is a lot. I know I just told you that you have a child. I know your work is important, but is it the only thing that's important?"

"I'm not saying that." Brady closed his eyes and sighed. "What do you want from me, Maggie?"

Everything. The thought startled her into silence. She bit the inside of her cheek and tightened her lips. Romantic dreams were for other people. She had to be rational. "I'd rather not tell her about you at all if we can't work out something definitively."

"I found out I have a daughter ten minutes ago. I'm dealing with the information as best I can." He looked at the photo of Amber and his eyes softened. "I want to do what's right, but I'm eight years too late. Tell me, what should I do?"

Maggie uncrossed her arms and laid her hand on top of his. His heat gave her comfort. She knew what Amber needed, what Amber deserved. What Maggie wished she'd had from the father she barely remembered. She took a deep breath before meeting his eyes.

"Two weeks. Give us two weeks of your time. Let Amber get to know you and adjust to having you in her life. If you decide you only want to be around occasionally after that—" Maggie swallowed the lump forming in her throat "—we can work something out."

His lips tightened into a thin line and she wondered if he would try to bargain more with her. He let out his breath in a puff. "I'll have to work while I'm there…"

Joy welled within Maggie, but it was tainted with concern. What if he didn't love Amber the way she deserved to be loved? What if he decided he didn't want to be a daddy to their daughter? What if Maggie accidentally drove him away and Amber hated her for the rest of her life?

She shook the doubts from her head. "We'll make it work." Realizing she held his hand, she released him and tucked a stray hair behind her ear.

"I'll need a few days to straighten things out, but then we can head back," Brady said.

Maggie's smile slipped as she focused on what Brady was saying. "We?"

"You don't think I'm going to let you go without me?" His half smile reminded her of the high school Brady she'd known. It was the same smile he'd given her when he'd caught her staring at him during gym class. The clanking of plates pulled her out of the small bubble she'd been in, bringing her back to the diner. Back to reality.

The reality was she needed to go home. "My plane ticket is for tomorrow. I have work and I need to take care of Amber—"

"All important details, but Sam obviously owes us. My assistant can take care of the ticket."

"I can't afford to stay at the hotel another night—"

"Stay with me." He cleared his throat. "I meant stay at my apartment."

The background noise faded again as she met his eyes. If only she were eighteen and willing to throw caution to the wind, to have one more night in Brady's arms. If only she'd let Penny pack her pretty nightgown. With her mother's illness and taking care of Amber, Maggie hadn't had time for anything else. She opened her mouth to say no, but the words stuck in her throat.

The girl she'd been would have been happy to let him take control of the situation, but now... "My flight is already booked. Penny is expecting me. Amber is expecting me. I should go home."

"I have a guest room," Brady said. "It will be easier if we head back together. That way you can make sure I get out of here. And you can get to know me better. You can fill me in on the last eight years."

"What do you mean?" Maggie asked, suddenly filled with nervous energy. Time alone with Brady Ward? Her inner teen-ager squealed with delight. She had to get ahold of herself.

"It's been years, Maggie." Brady sat back and looked for all intents and purposes to be a big-shot CEO as he stared down his fine nose at her. "We don't know each other that well. I've missed so much already. Birthdays, Christmases, her favorite color. All these things a father should know. I don't even know her birth date."

That twinge of guilt for her part in his missing Amber growing up picked at her conscience.

As if reading that she was wavering, Brady added, "You might decide I'm not the type of guy you want to bring home."

Given that he'd insisted that he wanted to meet Amber, Maggie suspected this was his way to make her feel comfortable with his plan by making it appear that it was in *her* best interest.

She wasn't eighteen anymore. Guilt or not. "And if I decide in the next few days that I don't want you to come meet Amber? You'd be fine with that?"

His eyes narrowed, but that cocksure smile of his told her that he had every intention of making sure that didn't happen. He leaned in conspiratorially and suddenly the air surrounding her was sucked away. "Of course. I'd respect your wishes. But you have to promise me something."

She returned his smile, wary but willing to play the game. "We don't make promises. Remember?"

His smile only faltered for a second. "That was years ago. Surely we can make a few promises now."

"Okay." She leaned away, ready to negotiate. "A promise for a promise."

He stroked his chin as he contemplated her. "You drive a hard bargain. Ladies first."

"You won't make any promises you can't keep to Amber. No promises of gifts or time unless you fully intend to live up to that promise."

Brady nodded. "Fair enough."

"And that extends to parenting," Maggie added.

"How so?"

"I've been with her these past seven years. You can come to visit, but she is *my* daughter. What I say goes."

"All right. No promises I can't keep and no going over your head on parenting." Brady's eyes twinkled mischievously though the serious look on his face never changed. "That sounds like two promises."

"Take it or leave it." Maggie shrugged. He'd either accept her decision or he could stay out of their lives. She expected him to ask for two promises, but instead he looked at her with something like…respect. Warmth blasted through her.

"Accepted." Brady moved in close and the diner faded into a distant rumble. "Now for your promise to me."

She squirmed in her chair. Whatever he was about to say she could walk away from if she needed to. She held that thought close to her heart as she gave him a nod to continue.

"You promise you'll give me a chance."

Her eyebrows wrinkled in confusion. "Would I be here if I wasn't ready to do that?"

"I don't know." Brady stroked his fingers along his jaw. "I don't know you any more than you know me."

"We grew up together," Maggie protested.

"We grew up *around* each other and except for one night, we never talked that much. We've both changed over the past eight years, Maggie."

He didn't have to remind her of that. Everything about him had changed. Clothes, hair, even his attitude. Eight years ago he'd had a haunted look about him. Even with his confidence, he hadn't been able to hide that look from her. For a brief moment, she'd met a kindred spirit and she'd let her impulsiveness get the best of her.

She definitely wasn't that girl anymore. Her first one-night stand had given her a daughter and a taste of responsibility she'd only toyed with before that. She was as firmly planted as the oak in her backyard.

"Give me a chance to get to know Amber and give her a chance to get to know me. Trust me to accept responsibility for this child I never knew I had. Trust me to try my best to not hurt Amber's feelings. Allow me to make a few mistakes without cutting me out of her life."

Could she trust him? What choice did she have? He was Amber's biological father. Maybe part of her had actually hoped he'd leave them alone and want nothing to do with them.

Maybe that's why it had been such a shock when Sam had delivered the money. Sure, Brady had been in London, but he probably would have wanted to be involved, somehow. Or maybe he would have been like Maggie's father and tossed her away.

"Maggie?"

She pulled herself from her past pain. This was a new future.

"Can you give me a chance?" Brady asked.

"I'll try." She gave him a halfhearted smile.

"And you'll stay with me until I can get away?"

How could she say no? She needed to get to know this man before she introduced him to her daughter. And she owed him the chance to learn about Amber.

"I don't know if this is a good idea." Insane was what it was; she was actually considering spending the next few days in Brady's apartment. Alone. With him. Certifiable. But if it meant Amber got to meet her daddy...

"It's a large apartment and I barely use it. I bought it as an investment." He glanced at his watch. "There's time to get your things and set you up in my apartment before my next meeting."

"You won't take no for an answer, will you?"

He winked. "Definitely not."

Chapter Five

One meeting rolled into the next, keeping Brady from focusing on the fact that he had a seven-year-old. Amber was never far from his mind as he went over the numbers with the team in London. Neither was Maggie.

When he finally managed to find time to sit at his desk, it was already quarter to five. On his return from lunch, he'd asked his assistant to order some groceries and have them sent to his apartment. As far as he knew, the refrigerator and cabinets were empty. The clock seemed to be marking every second he had left to get things straightened out. If he wanted to talk to Kyle before he left for the game tonight, Brady needed to get over to his office.

"Brady, I have those numbers you asked for yesterday." Jules appeared in his doorway. She looked up from the reports and frowned. "Are you going somewhere?"

Brady walked toward Jules. "Can you talk me through it on the way to Kyle's office?"

"Is there a meeting?"

"No." He waved off her concern. Though he knew in the past things had been done behind her back, that wasn't the way Brady worked. "I need to talk to Kyle about a personal matter before he leaves."

She nodded, though she still had a crease between her eyebrows. They started down the hall, and she handed him a page from the top of her papers. "I've been going through the preliminary budgets we set up. It looks like Peterson has made some changes without giving us notification."

Brady stopped abruptly and gave the sheet his full attention. Funds allocated to construction had been moved to another account. "Dammit."

"I can change it back, but—" She bit her lip and glanced at her watch.

This could take hours to resolve with Peterson and that's probably why he'd done it. If Jules went into his office now, she'd be in there for hours arguing about why it was correct in the first place. All the while, Peterson would be suggestive without being overt enough for her to press sexual harassment charges against him.

Brady took the papers from her. "I'll take care of it."

"Thanks." The tension drained out of Jules's face and shoulders. "I owe you."

"Don't think I won't hold you to that." Brady left Jules and knocked on Kyle's office door.

"Come in."

Kyle stood behind his desk, putting his laptop in his bag. His cell phone was cradled between his cheek and shoulder. He gestured for Brady to come forward.

"No…" Kyle said to the person on the other end of the line. "Thursday won't work. Yes, see you then."

He tucked the phone into its holder and gestured for Brady to take a seat. "If you'd been two minutes later, I would have been out the door."

"Glad I caught you, then." Brady took the offered seat and waited for Kyle to sit.

"What can I do for you today, Brady?"

Brady swallowed. "I know this is the worst timing, but I have a family emergency and need to take some time off."

Kyle leaned his elbows on the desk. "Is everything okay?"

"I honestly don't know." Brady chuckled, suddenly aware how absurd the situation sounded. "I recently found out I have a seven-year-old daughter who knows nothing about me. Her mother thought I knew, but I didn't."

"Congratulations." Kyle leaned back in his chair and it rocked with him. "So what were you thinking? A day? Two?"

Brady released the breath he'd been holding. "I have vacation built up, but I'm planning to continue working on the project while I'm in Illinois."

"How long?" Apparently, Kyle had noticed that Brady had dodged that question.

"Two weeks."

"Starting…"

"Tomorrow or the next day?"

Kyle templed his fingers to his lips as he contemplated Brady. The clock in the corner ticked mercilessly. Kyle's expression didn't change. Brady felt as if he were being silently quizzed on a subject he didn't know a single answer for.

Kyle stopped rocking. "You've just made a transition to this team. We usually like to build vacations into the schedule ahead of time." Kyle smiled. "But this qualifies as a family emergency."

"Great. I'll keep the Detrex project going via email and phone." Brady started to get up.

"No, the Detrex project is a huge account. Since Dave Peterson and Jules Morrison are both on the project, they should handle things while you are gone."

Brady sank back into the seat. If he let Peterson take over

the project, it would sink faster than the *Titanic*. Jules would have to deal with that scumbag every day. "With all due respect, Kyle, Peterson is a decent manager, but the contacts deal with me directly. We have so many balls in the air right now, one could drop and someone might not notice."

"Then you had better get them up to speed before you leave." Kyle rose from his chair, obviously dismissing him.

Brady stood. "Detrex is my project. I'd rather stay here than risk it failing because I left at the wrong time."

"The project won't fail without you." Again, Kyle dismissed his importance.

But Brady knew how this game was played. He'd studied it from every angle. He wasn't going to lose this project and the boost to his career. But if he let Maggie down this time, she might never let him see Amber.

"Let Jules lead it." Brady knew this was a risky move, but he had to play it. "If she has any questions, she can contact me or go to Peterson. It's only two weeks."

He hoped that Kyle would accept this. He could work the project with Jules while he was gone. Peterson wouldn't care if the project failed because it was Brady's and Jules's necks on the line. Until it's time to take credit.

"It's probably time Jules took on some additional responsibility." Kyle walked with Brady to the door and turned out the lights in his office. "But this project is too big to let fail. If I see any indication that she can't handle it, I will pass it off to Peterson."

Brady nodded. "Enjoy the game, Kyle."

Turning on his heels, Brady headed to Peterson's office. It was time to take his project back.

Within thirty minutes after Brady left, Maggie had finished putting away her things. What was she doing here?

She grabbed her phone off the nightstand and dialed Penny's number. It was early afternoon so she should be able to get her before Amber got home. "Did you tell him?" Penny asked immediately.

Maggie fell onto the bed. "Yes. I'm in his apartment right now. How is Amber doing?"

"She's fine. I'm fine. What are you doing on the phone with me?" Penny laughed. "I know it's been a while, but get out there."

"He went to work." Maggie rolled onto her side and stared out the window overlooking Central Park. "I told him."

"Okay." Penny stretched out the word as if trying to pick up the underlying meaning. "What happened?"

Maggie relayed the morning meeting followed by the nerve-racking lunch. And ended with her being dumped off in an apartment that looked like a pristine hotel room.

"It's like no one lives here." Maggie walked to the empty fridge. Her stomach rumbled, reminding her that she'd only eaten a few bites of lunch.

"Did you go in his room yet?" Penny sounded as if she was on the edge of her seat, waiting.

"I'm not going to snoop." Maggie turned to look at the closed bedroom door. She leaned against the refrigerator and wondered what he would have in his bedroom.

"I bet he has kinky sex toys."

"Penny!"

"Or naughty magazines."

"Seriously?"

Penny changed tactics. "Would you want someone like that around Amber? After all, it's important to have a good male role model and not all men can pass muster."

Maggie tapped her finger against her bottom lip. "He did say that he wanted me to find out about him before taking him to meet Amber."

"See?" Penny's triumph was obvious even hundreds of

miles away. "He *wants* you to snoop. Why else leave you in his apartment alone?"

"Because he had to go to work."

"Wrong!" Penny said, sounding like a buzzer. "Excuses, excuses. Get in there. I'll be right beside you. Make sure to use descriptive words like *black leather love swing.*"

"Okay, but don't get your hopes up." Maggie crossed the room and turned the doorknob. Just in case, she checked over her shoulder to make sure no one was in the apartment.

"A girl can dream."

Maggie shoved open the door and stepped into a room similar to her own. The hardwood floors from the living room continued into the room, providing the only warmth to the otherwise white, sterile room.

"Dying of suspense over here," Penny said.

"It's bigger than my room. King-size bed." No art. No photos. No spark of personality. Lifeless. Loveless. "Light tan bedspread with matching curtains. Black dresser. Two doors."

"One of them has to lead to the sex chamber." Penny's voice quivered.

"Do you think that if he had a sex chamber I would tell you?" Maggie rolled her eyes as she opened the first door to a bathroom.

"You'll tell me or I promise to read Amber Stephen King tonight."

"You wouldn't. Besides, I would be so shocked to find a sex chamber that I probably would tell you, so you could tell me what all the things were for."

"You know it," Penny said smugly.

"Door number one is a bathroom. Nice. Clean." Lifeless.

"I'll take what's behind door number two."

She opened the door to a walk-in closet the size of her bathroom at home. "Big closet."

The rich scent of sandalwood drifted over her as she entered the closet.

"Dirty mags?" Penny whispered, as if they were on the hunt together, instead of just Maggie waiting to get caught going through Brady's stuff.

The closet was neatly organized with nothing out of place. Suits lined up, next to neatly pressed pants, a few pairs of shoes. "It's as if he doesn't live here."

"That's it! Maybe he's a vampire." Penny snickered.

Maggie backed out of the closet and looked around for some evidence of anyone living there. "Worse, he's a workaholic. No one's house is this clean unless they don't live here."

"Or he stays at his girlfriend's." Penny's tone didn't help matters.

Maggie sank down on the edge of his bed. "I hadn't even thought about that. I didn't even ask. Why didn't I ask?"

"Because you were telling the dude he has a seven-year-old? I think you had more pressing things than 'are you dating?'"

"What if he is?" Maggie's heart clattered to a stop. She stood. "What if I'm getting in the way of his life here?"

"Whoa. Cart. Horse. Slow down, Maggie. It's only one possibility. As you said, this isn't about you hooking up with Brady. This is about Brady getting to know his daughter."

This wasn't about her. It was about Amber, and she shouldn't be in Brady's room at all. She rushed out and closed the door. "You were the one who wanted me to bring sexy nightgowns and bikinis."

Penny sighed. "Only because I want my friend back. The one before all the crap piled on her and made her into the glorious woman she is today. I love you, but you seriously need to get laid."

Checking to make sure she was alone, Maggie said, "I do

not need to get laid. I need to support my daughter and make sure her father is a decent man who won't let her down."

"You can do both, you know." Penny had been trying to get her to go out for the past several years. Saying it wasn't healthy for a woman in her twenties to be cooped up all the time. Between Amber and her mother, there hadn't been time to do the wild and crazy things that Penny did.

Maggie would never regret her daughter or the time she spent helping her mother. Given the choice, she would do it all over again.

"I can't do anything with Brady, Penny." The realization of what that would mean washed over her like a cold shower.

"Why not? He's there. You're there. You had a good time last time." Penny's voice was soft and coaxing.

Maggie let her gaze drift around the white-and-black room with its unused furniture. She squeezed her eyes shut and thought of her well-loved furniture that had been her mother's. She caught a hint of Brady's cologne, a warm rich scent in contrast to his surroundings. She opened her eyes. Regrets were a bitch.

"Because—" Maggie sighed "—if I ruin this for Amber, I'll never forgive myself."

Chapter Six

Brady scrubbed the weariness from his face as he rode the elevator to his apartment. Maggie would be waiting for him. It was such a foreign concept.

He hadn't had any kind of long-term relationship since he'd left Tawnee Valley. Only himself to worry about.

As he opened the door, he heard the sound of the television on low. He set his keys and BlackBerry on the side table. The curtains were all shut, blocking out the night skyline. By the flicker of the television screen he could see the table set for two and Maggie curled up on his couch.

She must've fallen asleep trying to wait for him. He should have told her not to bother. It hadn't crossed his mind to call. He always worked late. Checking the kitchen, he found the groceries he'd ordered, and in the fridge were two wrapped plates of food.

It stirred something in him that hadn't been touched in a while. Something he'd forgotten he wanted, but he couldn't quite name it. Warmth settled in his chest, pushing away the coldness of the New York fall evening. Some guys could work all the time and have a home life. Brady had never considered it. Too many ties, not enough mobility.

He strode over to the couch and squatted in front of Maggie. His future was tied to hers through Amber. Her hands were tucked under her cheek. In sleep, the tension around her was gone.

She was beautiful. Every time they touched, sensation rushed through his body. Could it just be an echo of attraction based on their shared past?

"Maggie," he whispered, almost afraid to wake her.

Her nose crinkled in response, and she tried to snuggle deeper into the couch.

He glanced at the table. He'd been a fool to think he'd have any time for getting to know about Amber or that Maggie would get a chance to know him. Work had always come first.

Peterson had been adamant the figures were incorrect. They'd argued over the numbers for five hours. Once they'd come to an agreement, Brady had written a detailed email to both Jules and the team that explained the changes. He would need all day tomorrow to catch Jules up on the state of the project and what needed to be done.

Complications, all of them. And yet, even knowing that Maggie waited, he hadn't been willing to let any of them drop. What kind of father would he be if he did that to his daughter? Was he even suited to being someone's father?

"Maggie?" he tried again. Still no response.

He went to his room and searched the upper shelf of his closet for the quilt he'd kept. The cotton was worn in spots, but it always felt warm in his hands. The patterned fabric seemed out of place in his apartment in London and even now, it was a misfit for his lifestyle.

When he returned to Maggie's side, he shook it out and gently laid it over her. Children had never been part of his plan. Maybe a wife who would have her own career to deal with, but never a child who would suffer from his lack of attention.

After getting a beer, he settled into the armchair and flipped the channel on the television. He should be in bed exhausted, but it felt good having someone else here. Maggie being here felt good. Most women would have waited up to ream him a good one for staying out late. Maybe he still had that to look forward to when Maggie woke.

Maggie stretched beneath the quilt and rolled onto her back. Her eyes blinked open and tried to focus on him.

"Hi." She sat up, rubbing her eyes. "What time is it?"

"Midnight." Brady held the bottle between his hands as he leaned his elbows on his knees. "I should have called."

Her sleepy smile made him forget to breathe. "I didn't expect you to."

Would she have expected him to if they were more than strangers? But they *were* more than strangers. He cleared the lump from his throat. "Did you want to eat?"

She nodded and started to rise, but froze when she saw the quilt. "This is gorgeous. Hand quilted. Where was this hiding? I didn't see it before."

Her smile dropped, and color rose in her cheeks.

"I mean…" She cut herself off with a groan and sank into the couch. "I shouldn't have, but Penny…"

"It's okay, Maggie." Brady stood and offered her his hand. "It's not like I have corporate secrets lying around my apartment."

He helped her up but didn't let go. Her body's warmth reached for him like a lover's embrace.

"What you see is what you get." Brady wasn't sure if he was trying to warn her off or make it clear that he didn't have anything to hide.

She cleared her throat. "I should have asked before snooping around."

Her gaze lifted to his and it felt like that night again. Energy pulsing between the two of them. Before there had been cattle lulling and the distant howls of coyotes as the backdrop, not the theme from *Law & Order*. He wanted to pull her in those last few inches and kiss her. To see if the spark between them could be coaxed into a fire. But he didn't. He'd never been one to shy away from attraction, but Maggie was different.

She blinked and stepped back. Busying herself with folding the quilt, she said, "I made dinner, but wrapped it up so when you got home, it would be ready."

He didn't know what to say. How could he think of sex when she was vulnerable in his apartment. With nowhere else to go in the middle of the night. She wasn't some random woman or coworker. This was Maggie Brown, resident of Tawnee Valley, his brother's classmate and the mother of his child. The type of girl you settled down with, and his commitment was to his work and his new life in New York.

She draped the quilt over the couch back and went to the kitchen.

His fingers itched to put the quilt away. To hide that piece of Tawnee Valley he'd kept. A memento of better times. He picked up the end, intending to pull it from the couch back.

"Penny was okay with staying an extra day or two. Amber only insisted I bring home something spectacular," Maggie said from the kitchen.

Brady forgot about the quilt. "Hopefully, I don't disappoint her."

"I think she meant a souvenir like a snow globe." Maggie reappeared with the two plates of food and set them on the table. "I'm not sure what to tell her about you."

Brady held out a chair for her, and she took the offered seat.

"What have you told her?" The aroma of fried chicken stirred his taste buds. Potatoes and vegetables rounded out the meal. His stomach rumbled. "It's been forever since I had fried chicken."

"I hope you like dessert because I made cookies, too. Idle hands and all that." She shrugged her shoulders as if embarrassed.

"I should have told you I would be late." Brady bit into a piece of chicken. He couldn't contain his moan of pleasure. He never would have guessed he missed good country cooking. "Heaven."

Maggie flushed with pleasure. "Thank you. Amber hasn't asked about her father too much."

"But when she does?"

"I don't know. I tell her that her father lives far away."

"Which is true." Damn Sam for his interference. Not that it would have changed much. His work had been in England and hadn't left room for a family. Even now he had no idea how he could work a child into his life, but he had to try.

Maggie met his gaze with sincerity. "I wasn't bitter about it. It was what it was. You weren't in the picture, but I wasn't going to bad-mouth you to someone who loves you whether she's met you or not."

"She loves me?" Brady couldn't keep the wonder from his voice. His family had always been a unit. Mother, father, two brothers. He'd never had the opportunity to question whether his parents would be there for him or if he wouldn't love them if they weren't. "Does she say that?"

"She doesn't have to." Maggie folded her hands together and he could see an inner battle being fought.

"Why is that?" He wasn't sure she'd answer, but it seemed to be what she was struggling with. Maybe searching for the words.

Finally, she raised her head to face him. "Because no mat-

ter what, a little girl has faith that her father, wherever he is
wants her and that whatever is keeping him from her mus
be important."

The carefully chosen words made Brady want to question
Maggie's relationship with her father. Mrs. Brown had been
on her own, but since his mother hadn't been one for gossip
and preferred to keep to the farm, he didn't know as much
about everyone in their small town as some people. Thi
overwhelming urge to protect Maggie rose within him. Had
her father hurt her?

He opened his mouth, ready to grill her for the details so
that he could right her wrongs, but Maggie hadn't come to
him. She wasn't offering *herself* to him.

"I hope I earn that trust." Brady broke the eye contact and
returned to eating.

"I'm sure you'll do fine." Maggie took her plate into th
kitchen. He could hear the faucet running. "Do you wan
cookies now or later?"

What could he say or do to make things right? He stood
and headed for the kitchen. Unfortunately, Maggie was head
ing out at the same time. He caught her shoulders as they ra
into each other.

"I—" she started, but stopped herself. Her warm, hazel
eyes gazed at him. He could almost smell the fresh-cut grass
the fragrant flowers growing wild, surrounding them. Eigh
years ago, she'd kissed him, offering him a taste, tantalizing
him with the promise of nothing more than a night.

He wanted to kiss her and it had a little to do with the nos
talgia that she evoked in him and everything to do with the
sexy woman she'd become. She didn't seem aware of her own
sexuality. Maybe he was overworked, maybe he had put too
little priority on his sex life, because right now, he longed
for Maggie to give him an offer like that one night. But wha
good would that do? No strings attached was what had lef

Maggie alone for eight years. But right now, he wanted another stolen moment with her.

Her hands came up on his chest. His heartbeat quickened. Could she feel it below her fingertips? Her lips parted and he couldn't resist the temptation any longer.

He lowered his head slowly, giving her ample time to smack him, run screaming to her room or ask him what in the world he was thinking. Instead, she rose up on her toes and met him halfway.

Her lips were soft under his and her arms clutched around his neck, drawing her body in close to his. Soft curves melted into him as lust hit him hard below the belt. It was all he could do to keep his hands planted on her shoulders.

When she made a little noise of need in the back of her throat, his brain went into meltdown. His hands flowed down her sides until they reached the bottom of her sweater.

Her breath hitched as he touched the skin at her waist. He pulled away from the kiss and met her gaze. His fingers lightly brushed along her sides under the sweater. Giving her every opportunity to stop him and hoping she wouldn't.

Maggie didn't look away, could hardly breathe. Her heart pounded in her chest and her insides had turned molten. *This shouldn't be happening.* Somewhere, little warning bells were going off in her head, but with his gaze on her, she felt as mesmerized as a deer caught in headlights.

His every touch left trails of nerves quaking in its wake. It had been so long since she'd been with a man. With a child and her mother to take care of, she hadn't had time. And pregnancy had scared her out of one-night stands.

But she'd always had a soft spot when it came to Brady Ward. He was definitely the exception and not the rule. Her breath caught when he finally cupped her breasts. She pulled his head down so she could recapture his lips with hers.

His hands lowered to her hips and without breaking li
contact, he started maneuvering her toward his bedroom. A
the while his fingers played with the waist of her jeans as he
fingers threaded through his hair.

Thinking was not allowed. With the flush of heat buildin
within her, it was a wonder she didn't combust on the spo
He stopped at his bedroom door.

He nipped at her lip as he lifted his head. "This is insane

"Completely." She pressed her body into his.

"We don't know anything about each other." He pushe
open his door and stepped her across the threshold.

"Didn't stop us before." Maggie laughed. It felt good. H
felt good. Life was a million miles away. Consequences wer
things best handled in the morning.

"One would think we had better judgment now," he mu
tered against her lips. He lifted her sweater off and tosse
it on a chair.

His gaze traveled over her and a moment of anxiety surge
through her. She wasn't a perky eighteen-year-old anymore
Fighting the urge to cover herself, she let him look at her.

"More beautiful than I remember." He lowered his hea
and kissed the top of each of her breasts.

Warmth pooled in her chest at his praise and his kisse
"More suave than I remember."

"I've had a little more practice." His fingers began to wor
on her jeans.

She tried to unbutton his shirt. Frustration bit into her a
the buttons refused to come undone. "I'm sadly out of prac
tice."

His lips claimed hers and she completely forgot what sh
was trying to do. Within moments, she felt him shrug out c
his shirt and her skin was touching his. Desire flooded her

"This wasn't exactly what I meant by getting to know m
better." Brady kissed the side of her throat.

She wanted to purr with contentment, to let him take the lead and show her how hot passion could burn. "This is a good way to judge someone's character."

Her hands skimmed over his back. Every muscle twitched under her fingers as they passed. Some sane part of her brain kept intruding. Was she going to have sex with Brady Ward? Why shouldn't she enjoy herself like Penny always insisted? Why shouldn't she let herself go for one night before returning to reality? *It's not real. It's New York.*

Tawnee Valley seemed forever away. Brady's mouth was magical as it pressed against her skin. She wanted to sink into this and forget everything. Escape.

His mouth found hers and she released her thoughts like balloons. Her knees hit the side of his bed. A flash of reasoning rushed through the fog gathered in her brain and the thought balloons crashed all around her.

She put her hands against his chest and pushed a little. He backed off immediately, but his hands held her hips against his.

"Too fast?" The concern in his eyes made her want to yell no, but instead, she nodded. He rested his forehead against hers and drew in a deep breath. "I kind of got carried away."

"Me, too," she admitted, even as her fingertips tingled with the touch of his hard chest beneath them.

He lifted his head and tipped her chin. His eyes searched hers. "It's been a long time since we've been here."

"We don't know each other at all." She sighed. His blue eyes had always been devastating to her. "We shouldn't be doing this."

"I understand." He pulled her into his arms and hugged her tight. Her cheek rested against his heart. There was nothing sensual about the hug, but she could feel his desire pressed against her. Her insides pulsed, but she ignored the craving.

"I should probably go to my room now," she said weakl*
Tell me to stay, a little part of her whispered.

He released her and stepped away. "I suppose that's f*
the best."

Trying to play it cool, she retrieved her sweater. She pr*
tended not to hear the little rumble from his chest as sh*
pulled it on. It felt good to be desired, even if she should fo*
get about it entirely.

"Tomorrow is Saturday…" She waited for him to acknow*
edge her, but didn't dare look his way as she walked towar*
the doorway.

"Unfortunately, I have to work all day."

She glanced back and he caught her gaze. For a momen*
she wanted to toss her cares to the wind. They'd had sex be*
fore. The only difference now was they had a connection i*
their daughter. *Their* daughter. She couldn't afford to sta*
anything with the father of her child, as ridiculous as tha*
sounded.

"We should be free to leave on Sunday." He stuffed h*
hands in his pockets, drawing her attention away from h*
eyes and over his chest, down his flat abs to the unbuttone*
fly of his pants.

She raised her eyes before venturing lower. "I should g*
to bed. It's been a long day."

"Maggie?"

She paused and he walked to her, stopping just out o*
arm's reach.

"You could stay in here. We could just talk. We don't hav*
to…"

A sigh worked its way through her. "I don't think that*
a good idea."

His grin had a sheepish quality about it. "You're probab*
right. Good night, Maggie, and thank you."

"For what?"

"For raising our daughter on your own. For flying here to ell me. For staying. For dinner. For being you."

"Good night, Brady." She gently closed the bedroom door behind her before she changed her mind.

Chapter Seven

Sunday morning, Brady sat at the table with his coffee. Maggie either wasn't awake yet or was still in her bedroom. During work yesterday, Brady had made progress and had packed the necessities from his desk: laptop, cell phone, wireless router. This might not be the best move for the project, but meeting his daughter was essential. When he'd walked into his apartment last night, he'd almost turned around to check the number to make sure he was in the right place.

The quilt remained on the back of the couch. A couple of framed photos sat on the table he threw his keys on. He recognized the frames as a Christmas gift from a work party.

He sat at his table scrolling through emails on his Black-Berry, trying to ignore the centerpiece of flowers in a vase he was fairly certain was new. The changes had made the room feel a little more like home and less like a hotel. Instead of making him feel good, it made him feel like a guest in his own space.

Except in his bedroom. A red silk scarf had been draped

over the foot of the bed, adding a bright spot of color to his drab existence. He had wanted that color to be Maggie draped in red silk across his bed. It even had a hint of her light floral scent to it. Positive she was already asleep last night, he'd made himself pass her door without knocking. But his imagination had kept him awake into the early morning.

"Good morning." Her voice startled him out of his thoughts. The real Maggie was better than his imagination. Her blond hair was damp. The green "I heart N.Y." T-shirt lovingly hugged her curves. His fingers itched from the memory of touching those curves. The scent of her strawberry shampoo floated around him. Far from the seductive scents of the tailor-suited women he was used to. Maggie had him uncomfortably aroused even in her cheap shirt with clean, unstyled hair.

"Morning," he mumbled. This was going to be a long two weeks. Being with her and unable to kiss her was going to be torture. She'd only said it was too fast. Not that she didn't want him. Was she leaving an open window?

"I only packed enough clothes for the weekend." Maggie held out the bottom of the T-shirt and looked at it. "It's not like I could run around naked. I bought this and two more for only ten dollars."

His mind stumbled and held on to the word *naked.* Damn lack of sleep. He shook his head to clear the image as she passed the table on her way to the kitchen and coffeemaker.

"I hope you don't mind the pictures. I found the frames in the guest bedroom closet and had the pictures of Amber with me. They were some I'd sent you over the years."

He could hear her moving around in his kitchen. So domestic. "They are fine."

"I couldn't help it." She leaned against the door frame with a cup of coffee cradled in her hands. Her gaze took in the room. "I know you don't have time, but my mom always said a little color makes life better. Of course, sometimes she got a little carried away with color. I haven't worn that red scarf she got me. Penny must have snuck it in my bag when I wasn't looking."

"We should be able to fly out today." Brady made himself focus on logistics and not the bit of skin peeking out from below her shirt. "My assistant was able to book two tickets on a flight leaving late this afternoon. After we pack, we can grab lunch before heading out."

She sat next to him at the table. Her focus stayed on the coffee cup. "We haven't discussed what's going to happen when we get to Tawnee Valley."

"We can discuss that now."

"We have an extra bedroom, but I'm not sure if I'm ready for you to stay with us." She met his gaze.

"I understand." Brady hadn't thought it through. The only time the two of them had been alone, he hadn't been able to keep his hands off her. He had slept like crap with her a door away for two nights. But he was sure she was thinking of Amber and not the attraction between them.

"I know there aren't any hotels nearby, unless you want to stay in Owen…"

"No, that would take too long." Owen was ten miles away and though the commute wasn't horrible, occasionally a tractor would slow traffic to a crawl, turning the ten minutes to twenty minutes or longer.

Maggie flushed. "I suppose if it's the only option…"

"I can stay with Sam." Brady's chest tightened. "He owes me at least that much for keeping this from me."

The lines of worry faded from Maggie's face and her pretty smile returned, making the bands around his chest ease. "That would be great."

"I'm sure Sam and I have a lot to discuss." Brady stood and took his cup to the sink. "I need to pack and answer a few emails. I'll send a quick email to Sam to expect me. Maybe we can go out and wander a little before our flight."

Because if they stayed here any longer with her smiling like that at him, he wouldn't be responsible for his actions. This attraction was temptation in the flesh. Briefly he thought if they got it out of their systems maybe the tension would go away. Or make it worse.

The ride to Tawnee Valley was a lot more comfortable than Maggie's trip to New York. Brady had booked them in first class. When she'd complained about the cost, he'd said they were the only tickets left.

Now she was sitting in a BMW heading down the highway that led to her small-town life. Maggie couldn't contain her excitement. New York had been intimidating, but she'd managed. It was time to return to Amber and their home.

They'd spent the remainder of their morning in New York wandering through Central Park. With Brady by her side, she hadn't worried like she had the day before. She even relaxed and enjoyed herself. They had chitchatted about this and that. He had asked question after question about Amber. Maggie had answered as best she could. It had been almost easy to ignore the little jolts she got when he put his hand at the small of her back to guide her.

Lunch had been simple and delicious and she could see the appeal of having lots of restaurants within walking distance. But she wouldn't give up the closeness of their community for the anonymity of the city for anything.

The plane ride had brought back the tension. Sitting close to him for two hours had been excruciating. Her body had hummed from the brush of his arm. Maintaining the conversation without wanting to kiss him when he was so close… she was lucky the seat hadn't combusted.

"Not much has changed around here." His voice drew he
to the present.

"No, not much," she agreed.

They'd been avoiding eye contact for most of the day. I
she looked at him, he looked away. If he looked at her, she
looked away. It was crazy, childish. They were the parents o
an amazing little girl, but trying to define their relationshi
with each other seemed impossible.

They'd passed through Owen a few minutes ago and wer
a few miles from Tawnee Valley. The plan was for Brady t
drop her off, but should she introduce him to Amber or wai
until they could set up a time so Maggie had time to prepar
Amber for her father? Maggie's heart went full throttle an
the snack from the plane sat like a lump in her stomach.

Before she knew it, they were stopping in front of he
house. What did he think of their town now that he'd live
in England and New York?

"Where do we go from here?" He caught her gaze. Hi
eyes were so blue.

She'd told Penny she wouldn't want Brady, but boy, ha
she been wrong. It had been too long. The other night hadn'
helped. It had stirred all those physical needs she'd ignore
while she took care of a growing child and her mother.

"Maggie?"

What she wouldn't give for another kiss. But the cost wa
too high. For her and for Amber. Amber needed her father
Maggie took in a deep breath and raised her eyes to his
"Why don't you come in? The sooner we get this over the
better, I think."

A wrinkle appeared on his forehead as if trying to fig
ure out what was in her mind. Good thing he wasn't a min
reader, because her thoughts were less than pure.

"If you think that's what's best," Brady said.

"Definitely." She pushed out of the car and waited by the

trunk until he opened it for her. She reached for her suitcase, but he beat her to it.

"I've got it."

She nodded and turned stiffly to walk toward the house. What on earth was she going to say to Amber?

Brady didn't have any trouble ignoring the sexual tension between Maggie and him as they approached the house. Nervousness filled him. This wasn't a baby he was meeting for the first time. This was a child. His child. Who had had seven years to build up in her mind what her daddy was like.

Now that he was here, he wasn't sure he could do this. Maybe he should tell Maggie that they'd do it tomorrow. That way he could worry about it through the night and formulate a plan. He reached out to grab Maggie's arm.

A screen door slammed and small footsteps raced down the wooden porch. A streak of purple and black slammed into Maggie. Maggie grabbed her daughter and swung around in a circle.

"I missed you, Mommy." Her voice was beautiful like the whisper of wind on a warm day.

"I missed you, too, baby." Maggie tucked her face into Amber's shoulder.

Brady felt as if he was intruding on a moment, as if he shouldn't be there, but he would never forget how beautiful the two of them looked together. Amber had his dark, almost-black hair but her smile was her grandmother's.

Maggie set Amber on the ground and knelt before her. Amber peeked around her and gazed at Brady with familiar blue eyes. A lump formed in his throat and his chest tightened. Warmth surged behind his eyes. He tried to smile, but he wasn't sure it came through.

"Amber, I have someone I want you to meet."

Amber glanced at her mother and back at Brady. She edged

in closer to Maggie and took her hand. The lump descended into Brady's gut like a lead cannonball. His own daughter didn't know him.

Maggie stood and turned. She took a deep breath, which reminded him he needed to breathe. "Amber, this is—"

"Brady." He stopped her from saying *your father*. "I'm Brady Ward. A friend of your mom's."

Maggie cocked an eyebrow at him. He shrugged. He wasn't ready to deal with being her dad and this way, Amber could decide if she liked him without worrying about him being the father who had never been there for her.

"You have a funny name, Mr. Ward." She peered at him with those gorgeous wide eyes and he couldn't believe that this was his daughter.

"You can call me Brady." He held out his hand.

She took his hand and jerked it up and down before releasing it. "It's nice to meet you."

She turned her back on him and looked up at her mother. Her whole face lit and her body trembled with excitement. "Did you bring me something?"

"Let's go inside. Maybe we can order a pizza, and you can get to know Brady better." Maggie glanced at him for confirmation.

"That sounds great." Brady nodded and followed them up the steps.

Maggie kept throwing confused looks over her shoulder at him. He wished he could explain, but for the first time in years, he felt completely out of control. He had no idea what Amber would say when she realized he was her daddy. Would she instantly like him or instantly hate him? He'd never been there for her. Birthdays, Christmas, the days that mattered and the ones when nothing happened. He hadn't been there. How could he look her in the eyes and say he was here now? What if she didn't believe him? Or what if work pulled him away before he was ready to leave? It was a risk he wasn't ready to take.

The porch steps creaked under his feet, and flecks of paint littered his path. He followed them into the small Victorian and was engulfed in warmth. All around was evidence of a house well loved by the occupants. Pictures of generations of family members were strewn all through the entryway and living room. A rainbow of colors collided anywhere he looked, but the mismatched furniture all seemed to blend together.

"Where would you like me to put the suitcase?" Brady asked.

"Brady Ward." A feminine voice brought his attention away from Maggie and Amber's reunion.

He would need to get used to these voices from his past if he was going to spend the next two weeks in Tawnee Valley. A copper-haired woman came down the narrow staircase. Her outfit hugged every curve, and her style hadn't changed much since high school. "Penny Montgomery?"

"Figures it would take Maggie to go and get you to come for a visit." Penny grabbed him into a hug and whispered in his ear, "You hurt either of them and I will personally lop off any dangly bits you have."

She pulled away. Her smile convinced him she'd be willing to do just that and she'd enjoy doing it. He pulled a tight smile. He hadn't even considered all the people he would run into while in Tawnee Valley. Maggie was the next victim of Penny's embrace.

"You know Brady, too?" Amber asked from behind Maggie.

"Yeah, we all went to school together." Penny knelt next to Amber and whispered something in her ear.

Amber giggled behind her hand and the sound softened the knot of resentment that had begun to form in Brady's chest.

If he hurt them like Penny said, it wouldn't be intentional. He was confident that if he stepped out of line, Maggie would make sure he knew it.

"No more secrets, you two." Maggie took her suitcase and opened it on the table. "Penny, can you order us all a pizza?"

Penny left the room but not before throwing Brady a serious look that said, "I'm watching you."

Just what he needed— another set of eyes watching him. Tawnee Valley was a small enough town. Being back and hanging around Maggie and Amber meant gossip was going to fly. He wouldn't have long before some well-meaning person spilled the beans accidentally to Amber. The speculation he could deal with, but Amber being hurt by it was a whole other story.

"Tell me about New York," Amber said to Maggie as she knelt in one of the chairs near her mother. Her purple gem earrings sparkled in the overhead light. She peered into the bag, looking to find what Maggie had brought her.

Brady should have gotten her something. Would that have been odd? For a friend of her mother's, maybe. Not odd for a father. Dammit, why didn't he let Maggie tell her? Did he think it would be better this way? Was he already screwing things up?

"Brady lives there and before that he lived in London, England." Maggie glanced at him and he saw all the encouragement he needed in her eyes. Maggie seemed to have a spark of faith in him even if Penny didn't.

"You lived in England?" Amber's full attention was on Brady.

"Yes, I did. For eight years."

"I'm almost eight. Did you meet the queen or the prince?" Before he could answer, Amber's attention was drawn away when Maggie held out a plastic bag.

"For you."

Amber quickly unwrapped the snow globe of the Statue of Liberty and the New York skyline. "Thank you, Mommy!"

She shook it and watched the snow fall and swirl. After a couple more times, she shyly lifted her gaze to Brady and he felt his heart sing. "Would you tell me about England?"

"Of course," Brady said.

While they waited for pizza, Brady told Amber all about England, answering the silly questions and the serious ones with complete openness. Maggie watched them with an expression he couldn't read. His daughter was curious, intelligent and everything he could have ever hoped for. If he had hoped for a child.

His career was his life. Work was what he'd return to when these weeks were finished. Work was what would keep him from coming around for every little event in Amber's life.

Work kept him sane, and he was making a difference. Part of him wished he could be that father that grilled on Sundays and played catch and wiped away tears, but that wasn't who he was. As he looked into the innocent eyes of his daughter, he knew he'd better not forget that and start to wish for more. This was all he was capable of.

Chapter Eight

Maggie washed the pizza dishes while Brady told Amber an English story with princes and princesses. He had looked anxiously at Maggie—for approval or strength, she wasn't sure— but she'd smiled softly and nodded. He must have found what he needed as he started a tale of jousting.

This was everything she'd always hoped for in a reunion with her father, but she knew it wouldn't have been the same. Her father had left her. He'd known about her from the beginning and one day got sick of being someone's daddy. Maybe Brady would get sick of it, too, and she'd be left with a broken-hearted daughter. Maybe it was better to not tell Amber who he was. Let her think he was some stranger from Maggie's past who happened into their lives.

"Are you doing okay?" Penny asked from the doorway.

"Yeah." Maggie swiped at a strand of hair. "It's weird, right? Brady being here? With her?"

Maggie couldn't help the anxiety cascading through her

system. She didn't know whether to be happy or sad or worried that Amber had finally met her father.

"You didn't tell me what happened in New York." Penny grabbed a towel and began to dry the dishes.

"There isn't anything to tell. He worked. I waited." *Except that one night when we almost wound up in his bed.* Her knees went a little loose thinking about his lips on her neck.

"I don't believe you, but I'll let it go." Penny took the next dish. "Is he staying here?"

"No, he's staying with Sam." Maggie glanced over her shoulder toward the living room where she could hear Amber laughing. "This is good."

"I sure hope so. Do you want me to stick around?" Penny made comically shifty eyes toward the door. She'd been at Maggie's house for a few days and probably had plans.

"No, we'll be fine. It's almost Amber's bedtime. Brady has to get out to the farm."

"Good, because I have a hot date." Penny grinned and slipped on her jacket.

"I don't think that your DVR counts as a date."

"You haven't seen *Supernatural.* Call me later." Penny kissed Maggie on the cheek. "If he does anything wrong, you tell me and I'll take care of him."

"I'm sure you will." Maggie dried her hands. She could handle Brady in Tawnee Valley.

After Penny left, Maggie finished cleaning before walking toward the voices in her living room. She leaned against the doorjamb, suddenly exhausted.

"Dragons roamed the streets, but Lady Jane was more than a match for them." Brady's voice had taken on a slight accent as he told the English story.

They sat facing each other, lost in their own little world. The same dark hair, the same blue eyes, the same slope of their noses. It would take a fool to realize they weren't father and daughter. Amber leaned forward, straining to listen to every word that came out of Brady's mouth.

Maggie remembered that feeling all too well. Even though he barely knew her in high school, she'd had the biggest crush on him. She'd spent hours doodling her name with his on her folders. It had been a silly, girlish crush.

When he'd left for college, she'd finally let herself believe it wasn't going to happen. He wasn't going to one day see her as anything more than a classmate of his brother's. She'd moved on to Josh. They were together until the end of high school, but it became clear they were going in separate directions and were better friends than lovers. And graduation…a hot summer night spent tangled in Brady's sheets, sheltered by his arms. No expectations. No regrets.

"There are no dragons in England nowadays. But the roads aren't much better." Brady looked up and caught her watching them. His eyes sparkled with happiness. Her heart stuttered. What she wouldn't have given back then to have him look at her like this.

She held her breath. Surely he could hear the rapid beat of her heart from over there.

"Mommy, Brady says that the English call rain boots wellies. Isn't that funny?" Amber's blue eyes were filled with wonder and joy.

Watching the two of them together, Maggie didn't regret bringing Brady into her home. Whether or not she'd regret it in two weeks, she had no way of knowing. After all, Brady hadn't come clean about being Amber's father. She needed to ask him about that. "It's about time for bed. Why don't you thank Brady for the stories and go shower?"

"Thank you," Amber said dutifully. "Are you coming back?"

"Of course. I'll be here for a couple of weeks." Brady kept his attention focused on Amber.

Maggie exhaled. She'd known he was going to stay, but maybe he didn't want to be with them every day. She couldn't expect him to, especially with work, but it had been part of their bargain that she give him a chance. Well, that couldn't happen if he wasn't around.

"You should stay with us. You could use Nana's room. Mommy cleaned it real nice and changed it into a guest bedroom. My nana went to heaven. She won't mind." Amber's expressions changed rapidly during her speech. She hadn't learned how to hide her emotions. With everything she'd been through, Maggie was grateful Amber hadn't grown up too fast.

Brady's mouth dropped open as if he wasn't sure what to say. "I'm going to stay with my brother for now."

"Okay." Amber raced over and hugged him around the waist. His hands went out to the side and he gave Maggie a look that said, "What do I do?" Before he could do anything, it was over.

Maggie smiled and got her own tackle hug before Amber raced upstairs, yelling over her shoulder, "I'll see you tomorrow, Brady."

Brady sank into the chair and rubbed his face.

"How are you holding up?" Maggie stayed where she was in the doorway. Afraid that if she got too much closer she'd want to touch him, and touching him might lead to things best not explored. Her fingers tingled. She knew exactly how tight his muscles were. As well-defined as his younger self.

"Tired." Brady laced his fingers together and hung his head. "This is going to be exhausting."

"She's usually not this wound up." Maggie stepped toward him, wanting to reassure him without scaring him off.

"It's not Amber." He lifted his gaze to hers.

For a moment she thought he was going to say it was her. That she was making him exhausted.

"It's this town."

She let out a sigh of relief.

He pushed himself to his feet and stalked over to the window. "I'd forgotten how soul crushing it is. It wasn't just my parents' deaths that made me want to run, but people like Penny. Everyone thought they were involved in everyone else's business."

Maggie bristled. "It's a community. We care for each other. Penny is protective of Amber and there isn't anything wrong with that. She was there for us."

"It's good to have someone look out for you, but this place is like a virus. Everything spreads quickly and not a thing can stop it." Brady turned back to her, and she could see the anger in his eyes.

"It's a good thing you don't have to live here." Maggie crossed her arms as her spine stiffened. "What time are you coming over tomorrow?"

"I don't mean you or Amber." His tone softened. "I just…"

"You don't want to be in Tawnee Valley. Completely understandable after you've spent the past eight years alone over in England." Damn him for making her care about him even an inch.

"I kept busy and kept my nose out of other people's business." Brady walked over to her until they were close enough to touch. "I don't need to be watched like a hawk or told when I'm out of line by anyone but you, Maggie. Amber is your responsibility and I won't begrudge that, but she's not this town's child and they have no say in what we do."

Her anger softened a little with his words. With him this close, it was like standing next to a live wire. She wanted to grab his shirt and kiss him. Finish what they'd started a few days ago. She breathed deeply and ended up filling her lungs with the scent of him—sandalwood and that underlying scent that was uniquely Brady.

He stepped closer, almost hesitantly, as if to give her the chance to push him away. The angry words faded into the background, just noise that hadn't mattered. Eight years dropped away in an instant and she felt eighteen again, at a crossroads that didn't have a good ending, no matter which way she looked. Her mother's diagnosis had meant staying home and helping her. There had been no other family to turn to, and they couldn't have afforded a nurse with the level of treatment her mother had needed.

For one night, she had wanted to feel free, uncaged. She'd wanted Brady. They had gone upstairs to his room with no backward glances. Every touch had been torture and pleasure, both of them knowing that when the morning came, it would be time to return to their lives as if nothing had happened between them.

"Maggie?" Her name tumbled from his lips and he leaned toward her, daring her to close the last bit of distance like she had in New York.

Her body swayed toward him as if it couldn't resist his pull.

"Mommy, I forgot a towel," Amber yelled over the noise of the shower.

Maggie tried to find something more in Brady's eyes, but the shutters fell and he stepped back.

"I'll be right up." Maggie didn't move. They weren't kids anymore. Both had responsibilities elsewhere, and their paths were only joined by one thing—Amber. That's all they had between them.

Brady cleared his throat. "What time does school let out?"

"Three." Maggie was glad the word came out without being breathless.

"Tell Amber good-night for me." He brushed past her and headed to the front door.

She sighed and let out a little shiver before turning to go upstairs.

"Good night, Maggie," he said softly as the door shut.

Brady stood on the front porch of his childhood home. A whole host of memories had swarmed in to greet him. From toddler to teenager, he'd spent many days on this porch, dreaming of a future far away. He'd loved his parents and wanted to make them proud, but farming had never been his passion.

He'd made sure to be the best at anything he tried. To be better at school and sports than his two brothers. It hadn't mattered. Sam was his father's favorite and Luke had been their mother's favorite. Not that Brady had been neglected. He'd been loved. He'd just been different. Never quite fit in.

As he was getting ready to knock, the door swung open.

"Brady." Sam moved out of the way to let him through.

So many emotions played through Brady's mind. Guilt, hurt, past resentment. Nothing compared to the anger for keeping Brady's daughter a secret.

"Sam." Brady rolled his suitcase into the dining room and shrugged off his laptop bag. Nothing had changed in the house. Sam had kept it exactly as Mom had left it. Everything had aged, though. What was once a cream-colored paint had yellowed. From here he could see that the kitchen vinyl was worn from years of boots treading across its surface. The place was clean but far from spotless.

"I made up your bed." Sam moved farther into the house, going through the doorway that led to the kitchen.

Brady closed his eyes and took a deep breath. It was as if he had only been gone for the school year and not eight years. He should have decked Sam when he answered the door, but nothing would come from a confrontation. Sam wasn't going to change.

From the kitchen came the sounds of a chair rubbing against the floor and a newspaper rustling. If Brady weren't emotionally drained from meeting Amber and dealing with Maggie, he might have gone in there and started in on Sam for his lies. Instead, Brady lifted his suitcase and climbed the stairs to his old room. The doorknob was still loose in the casing and made a metallic rattle when he opened it.

Exactly as he left it with the exception of the quilt. Brady had taken the quilt his mother had made for him when he left. Even though he'd felt compelled to leave everything behind and start a new life, he couldn't let go of such a simple thing as a blanket.

The double bed barely fit in the small room and left little room for the dresser. When he was fourteen, Mom had found the old bed frame at an auction.

As always, if Mom had wanted something done, the three of them would move heaven and earth for her. They'd managed to get the bed up the narrow stairs with a few bruises and a lot of cussing. Brady ran his hand over the smooth wood footboard. Now he barely spoke to his brothers. Luke kept in touch when he could. He had always been the mediator between Brady and Sam. But their lives were all so different and without Mom and Dad to draw them together...

Pushing the thoughts from his head, he quickly unpacked his suitcase and tucked it away under the bed. He hadn't worked at all today but since it was Sunday, it probably didn't matter.

He would have to find somewhere else to work. Sam had to have a computer hidden somewhere in this house, which meant there might be a decent desk and chair for him to work on.

Shouldering his laptop bag, Brady made his way downstairs. Anywhere he went in town, he would run into people from his past and his parents' past. Interruptions would eat into his work time.

He walked through the farmhouse, trying to ignore the memories floating on the edge of his mind and to concentrate on finding somewhere to work. The main difference in the living room was the fancy flat-screen TV and stereo components. Gone was the old tube TV console and rabbit ears. Their father had always complained that if you had time to sit, you had time to work. There were always chores to be done.

Obviously, Sam didn't feel the same way.

The little room had a meager office with an old dial-up modem hooked to the modern computer. Brady wondered if he could even get a signal for his wireless router this far down in the valley.

The metal folding chair and particle-board desk wouldn't be ideal for working long hours. Back in the dining room, Brady set his laptop on the table and stretched out his shoulders. He could hear the rustle of a newspaper from the kitchen.

If he told Sam off for keeping Amber from him, what good would it do? Sam had never listened to anyone but their father. In his mind, Sam had probably justified it with some bullshit he'd decided on when Brady had left.

No. Sam was one demon Brady wasn't ready to face yet. And given the silence from the kitchen, Sam wasn't ready, either. Maybe they never would be. Two weeks and Brady would be gone again. Nothing was going to change that. And nothing would change between them.

Chapter Nine

Maggie sat at her desk working on some bills for the furniture store while Amber did her homework at the kitchen table. Brady had brought in his laptop and sat next to Amber. Two minutes later, he'd answered a call on his cell phone and wandered out to the front porch.

"Alex Conrad puked in the hallway today. It was so gross." Amber tipped back in her chair to look around the door frame at Maggie.

"That sounds unpleasant. All four on the floor." Referring to the chair legs. Maggie looked at her watch again. Brady had been outside for the past thirty minutes. She'd begun to like the guy yesterday. He'd been attentive and helpful in the airport and the car ride to Tawnee Valley. He'd focused on Amber, answering her nonstop questions like a pro. Just when she thought he was going to give it a real go and leave the workaholic in New York, the New York Brady had shown up at her door jonesing for an internet connection.

She'd wanted to ask how it went with Sam, but he hadn't spared her more than a couple of sentences since he'd arrived.

"There were chunks—"

"That's enough, Amber Marie. Get back to your homework." Maggie finished the last check and started putting things away. "Maybe after homework and dinner, we can go get some ice cream."

"Yay!" Amber bent her head over the page of math problems.

Maggie carried the stamped envelopes out the front door. Brady stood on the far end of the porch, gesturing while he spoke intensely on the phone.

She walked to the mailbox and dropped the bills in. At least he was passionate about his work. What would it be like if he were that passionate about Amber? Would he even give a second thought to the phone when it rang? Would it have been better if Maggie had left it alone? If he'd never found out about Amber? It's not as if he would visit Sam and accidentally run into Amber and her. Besides, half the town thought Amber was Sam's. The other half thought she was Luke's.

"Don't let Peterson take over, Jules." Brady turned, and Maggie could feel his frustration like a heat wave. "We've worked too hard to let him step in and take the credit."

Maggie perched on the porch railing and crossed her arms, waiting for him to be finished with his conversation. She had a thing or two to talk to him about.

"Tell him no." Brady lifted his gaze.

Her body buzzed with energy as he met her eyes. Irritating attraction. It kept popping up when all she wanted to be was mad. He held up one finger to indicate one minute. She resisted the urge to hold up a different finger with a very different meaning.

"Fine. Tell him we're dating and that's the reason you guys can't go out."

Maggie's heart sank like a lead balloon crashing into her gut. Dating? It made sense. The Brady she'd known had rarely been without a girlfriend in school. He was smart, sexy and a good guy. She never would have guessed the Brady she'd known would be a cheater, but New York Brady was someone entirely different. If she hadn't stopped them, they would have had sex in New York. Thank goodness she'd come to her senses. He'd changed, and she had to remember that.

A different rant was forming in her head, but he wasn't here for Maggie. He was here for Amber. And right now, he was sucking at it.

"It'll be okay. Run the preliminary numbers again and cross-reference the new numbers. Email me the spreadsheet and I'll see what I can do."

Maggie shored up her defensive wall as she prepared to launch her attack. The bubble of heat welling within had nothing to do with the fact that he was a two-timing— She stopped her thoughts and drew in a breath. For Amber.

Brady hit a button on his phone and walked toward her.

When he stopped within touching distance, he looked worried. "Is something wrong?"

"Yes." She swallowed the hurt of finding out he was dating someone as hoity-toity as he was, and the fact her crush on him wasn't affected by that fact. Mother first. "Amber is expecting you to pay attention to her. I'm expecting you to put away the phone for the few hours you get to spend with her."

The worry fell off Brady's face. A little anger crept into its place. "This isn't exactly a cakewalk for me. I didn't ask for any of this and it isn't the best time to be away from the office. I have people relying on me."

Like Jules? The words pressed on her tongue to get out, but she clamped her lips shut.

"I promised I would get to know Amber, and I will." The muscle in his jaw ticked.

"Fine, but no more phone calls. You have all day to take them—you don't need to take them here." She kept her head up and ignored the heat his body stirred in her.

"I can't control when other people need to consult with me." He took a step forward. "That was part of the deal, too. I need to work while I'm here."

"While in Tawnee Valley, yes, but while at my house with my daughter, no." Maggie's heart stuttered against her chest. She hadn't spent the past eight years being brave to crumple under pressure now. She pulled her shoulders back and met his gaze with an uncompromising one.

Eight years ago she would have backed down. So in love with the idea of Brady Ward that she would have done anything he asked of her. But that girl had grown up and could face down anything and anybody. Having a baby out of wedlock wasn't as big a deal now, but with a small town, it hadn't been a *cakewalk,* as Brady put it.

She could almost feel the battle that waged between them. Will against will. She had the advantage. She had the power to stop him from seeing their daughter. His jaw was tight and he looked as if he was about to say something they might both regret.

She tipped her chin up another notch. "Promises or not. She is my daughter."

"She is *our* daughter." He straightened more, towering over her and inside she crumpled a little, but on the outside she remained a rock. "If I have to get a court-ordered DNA sample, I will. But since you don't deny that she is mine, it shouldn't come to that. As long as you don't make unreasonable demands of me, I won't make unreasonable demands of you."

She bristled. "I didn't *have* to tell you about her."

"But you did."

They stood close enough to touch, but neither of them

moved an inch. Neither willing to retreat. She wouldn't give on this one. "If you want to work, stay at the farm."

"Fine." The soft-spoken word caught her off guard.

"What?" Was Brady Ward giving in to her demands? Her confusion made her anger dissipate.

"I'm not going to fight you on this." Brady reached out and took her hand. His whole demeanor changed. The hard businessman shut down and the country boy reemerged. The charmer she'd been half in love with. "I'm here for a short time. If I can't be here one hundred percent for Amber, I'll stay out at the farm. Just don't lose faith in me yet."

Her pulse raced as he lightly held her hand in his. She hadn't won the war, but she'd won this battle. Giddiness filled her. The warmth of his touch caused her breathing to become uneven. The steel look had left his blue eyes until they became warm and she felt herself softening. Swaying ever so much closer.

He has a girlfriend! Her mind had to shout to remind her. Reluctantly, she took her hand back, resisting the urge to rub the tingles away. Just another reason to keep her distance. It would help her remember that Brady was here only for Amber.

She nodded, not trusting her voice. Fortunately, Amber came rushing out the door at that moment, keeping both of them from making a fool out of her.

As they stood in line at the ice cream shop after dinner, Brady couldn't understand why Maggie was still angry. Amber had kept up the conversation during dinner, but Maggie had been visibly upset. When Amber had asked Maggie if she was okay, Maggie had claimed to have a headache. But she'd given him a glance that made him believe he was the headache.

He had business to do. It wasn't as if he could take off

two weeks and not do his work, regardless of what his boss thought. And with the limitations of the internet out at the farm, he could only do so much there. But she didn't seem to understand that.

Besides, Amber had been busy with homework. It wasn't as though she needed his constant attention. Did Maggie expect him to help Amber with her homework? Because from what he'd seen so far, she didn't need it.

"I want the mint chocolate chip in a waffle cone with chocolate sprinkles and chocolate sauce." Amber bubbled over with excitement as she pointed her fingers against the cold glass.

"Keep your hands off the glass, please." Maggie avoided looking at Brady.

If that's the way she wanted it, fine with him. He would figure out how to bridge this gap between them eventually. Her eyes had softened after he'd given in and her lips had parted slightly. Temptation in the flesh. And then she'd gone cold and rigid. Obviously, even if she desired him, she didn't want to. Maybe he was reading her wrong. But he hadn't read her wrong in New York. She'd been as into him as he'd been into her. He mentally shook his head as he pulled out a twenty and handed it to the cashier before Maggie had a chance to dig in her purse.

That got a glare out of her, but he just smiled.

Right now he had to focus on getting to know Amber in the time he had left. As much as he desired Maggie, she needed someone who would be there for her. He wasn't ready for a full-time family.

An elderly man in ripped khakis and a plaid shirt sidled up next to Brady. "You know it's rude to not say hello to your elders."

Brady looked over and recognized Paul Morgan, a friend of his dad's. "When I see an elder, I'll be sure to say hi."

Paul took Brady's offered hand in a hearty handshake. Paul chuckled and gestured toward Amber and Maggie getting the ice cream they'd chosen.

"Good family you got there."

Brady hesitated. He almost said *they're not mine,* but that wasn't exactly true. Amber was his daughter, but Maggie wasn't his wife or his in any way. And at the rate they were going, they wouldn't even be friends by the end of the week.

Brady nodded, not knowing what else to do.

"You been over to see Sam?" Paul asked.

Brady looked at his feet before returning Paul's gaze. How much did he know about the blowup between the brothers? "I'm staying out at the old farm."

"Good that you two let bygones go. Sam's done a great job tending the farm. His livestock is the best in the county. And the way he took over raising you and Luke, that shows real courage. Shame your parents aren't around to see how well you boys grew up."

Even as the familiar burn of jealousy engulfed him from all the praise for Sam, Brady couldn't help but think of how disappointed his parents would be that he and his brothers weren't close like when they were young. His mother had always mended the fences between him and Sam when they fought, but she wasn't here now. Brady wasn't sure their relationship could be mended after what Sam did to Maggie.

"Looks like I should get back to…" Brady gestured to Maggie and Amber, not knowing what to call them. "It was good seeing you."

"You should stop for a visit while you're in town," Paul said.

Brady shook Paul's hand before heading over to the table Maggie and Amber had found.

Paul had a neighboring farm to the Wards'. Brady hadn't even asked how Paul's wife was doing. Or his farm or crops.

Mom would have scolded him for not showing common courtesy.

"Don't you want ice cream?" Amber's nose was coated with a skim layer of green ice cream. She looked at him with those adoring eyes and he melted inside. He did have one thing Sam didn't.

He patted his stomach as he sat. "I'm stuffed from that dinner your mom prepared. She must be the best cook in the tri-county area."

He glanced over at Maggie, but she didn't seem amused by his declaration.

He missed her smiles. And their absence made him try even harder to get one. Apparently, it was going to take more than complimenting her cooking.

"How was school today?" Brady asked.

"Alex puked all over the hallway. It was disgusting." Amber drew out the last word and made the requisite face to go along with it.

"That's what you remember from school?" Brady shook his head and tried to keep a straight face. He'd been expecting something about the math homework she'd had or the spelling test she'd mentioned earlier. Not some kid puking in the hall.

She took a bite of her cone. "It was the most exciting thing that happened all day. It almost splattered all over Jessica and Maddy. Everyone jumped out of the way while the janitor went and got kitty litter."

Brady smiled. "I suppose that would be exciting."

Amber continued to eat her green ice cream as if they'd been discussing art rather than vomit. From what Brady remembered of grade school, it probably would have been the highlight of his day, too.

He turned to Maggie to see how she was reacting. "How was your day today?"

Maybe she would answer a direct question.

"Fine." Maggie kept her gaze out the window past him.

"Anyone puke?" Brady winked at Amber, who giggled.

"Nope."

Nothing. He sighed internally. As he scanned the ice cream shop, people had a familiar look about them. But he'd been away for so long, he couldn't tell who they were.

He'd almost forgotten what it was like to be in a small town. To be recognized by who your parents were, where you'd gone to school and even whose pigtail you'd pulled when you were seven, and not by what you'd accomplished since then.

The other people in the ice cream store pretended not to be looking at them, but Brady wasn't fooled. They knew he was Brady Ward and he was with Maggie Brown and her daughter. If people hadn't put two and two together before, their being together would leave little doubt.

It bothered him that people would see that Maggie wasn't talking to him.

But it bothered him more that Maggie wouldn't meet his eyes. He didn't like that she wouldn't talk to him, except for in clipped words. And he didn't like the pressed thinness of her lush lips.

"Maggie?" he said.

She faced him with a questioning look in her eyes. None of the spunk that had drawn him to her years ago reflected in them.

What could he say to make her happy? To bring back that little smile she'd give him when he said just the right thing.

"I might be late tomorrow." Dumb, dumb man. That wasn't what he'd meant to say, but darn it all, he wasn't used to being around women in a nonwork environment. He wasn't used to someone counting on him outside of work projects.

Her eyes grew frostier, and she nodded briskly. He flinched internally.

"Amber, you need to go wash." She went back to ignoring him as Amber raced off to the bathroom.

Maybe over the years, he'd let his work consume him until work was all he had. There wasn't a separation between the relaxed him and the work him. It was how he protected himself. He couldn't let that go for a couple of weeks to "hang out." He *needed* to work, it had kept away the pain that he'd felt when his mother had passed so soon after his father. The anger and rage that had engulfed him; that had forced his hand and made him flee not a hundred miles away, but across an ocean.

In London, no one had asked him about his parents. No one had offered sympathy for his loss, because they hadn't known. Here, it was in their eyes and words, even if they never said it out loud.

As they walked home in the ebbing twilight, Amber rambled on about this and that. Brady couldn't get out of his head. It didn't help that Maggie continued her silent treatment. The street was lined with trees and though he hadn't walked this particular street much as a kid, it was familiar. Like every other street in Tawnee Valley. The past seemed to press in on him and force his hand in the present. He had nothing to give to anyone. What made him think Amber even wanted *him* for a father?

He had run away from the responsibility of being part of a family. He had run out on Sam and Luke—his own brothers. Even though Sam had been controlling, he could have used some guidance.

As they reached the porch steps, Amber spun around. "Do you want to see the scrapbook Nana and I put together?"

"Sure." Brady didn't know if Maggie wanted him to hang around any later, but he didn't want to leave. He wanted to be part of this family, part of whatever they were creating here. Tonight he didn't want to run.

Amber bounded into the house. The screen door slammed behind her. Maggie climbed a couple of steps before stopping. Brady barely kept himself from running into her.

"I need to know if you are in this." Maggie didn't turn to meet his gaze. The light from inside the house lit her profile, but he couldn't make out her expression.

"I wouldn't have come all this way if I weren't." He wasn't sure what she was referring to, but he could only assume this was a continuation of their earlier argument about work.

"Either you tell Amber you are her father or you don't, but I need to know what you are going to do. I can't keep lying to her." Finally, she turned to face him. On the steps she was the same height as him. In her eyes was the fierce protectiveness of a mother trying to keep her child from harm.

"I've done a lot of things since I left Tawnee Valley." Brady cleared his throat. "I've made a lot of deals and created thousands of jobs."

She crossed her arms over her chest and looked down her nose at him. Not impressed with his resume.

"But…" What could he say to convince her? Years of negotiating multimillion-dollar deals failed him.

"But what, Brady?"

He searched her eyes, trying to figure out what technique would work. Trying to assess the risks versus the rewards of each scenario, but this wasn't work. This was a little girl. His little girl.

"I'm good at what I do, but—" he shrugged and gave up trying to hide "—I suck at the emotional stuff."

Her face softened slightly, but her body remained tense.

He took a deep breath as if he were about to jump into a pool. "I don't know how to be a daddy."

She dropped her arms. "She needs to know you care about her. No one's asking you to be her daddy."

"But I want to be."

"You do?" Skepticism lingered in her expression.

He closed the distance between them. "I've missed so much already. I don't want to miss any more. Amber is an amazing kid." He paused. "Our kid."

"I haven't made my mind up about you yet."

He could tell that he was winning here. Even as he felt more exposed than he had ever felt. "What if she doesn't like me? What if her fantasy of her dad is built up so high in her mind that only Superman could fulfill her dreams?"

Maggie's eyes glistened with unshed tears. "All a little girl wants from her father is for him to be there for her."

"Was your father there for you?" he asked, pushing gently for more information. There was something there. He'd sensed it before.

She shook her head, and a tear escaped down her cheek.

He smoothed it away with his thumb. "I'll do my best to not disappoint either of you."

That small smile crept onto her lips and he wanted to shout his victory. Her smooth skin beneath his thumb sent electricity down his spine. His body tensed at the sudden flood of desire pumping through his veins.

"I know you won't." She placed her hand over his on her cheek.

Trust. Had he ever known anyone quite like Maggie Brown? From a starry-eyed girl to a sultry teenager to this glorious woman standing before him, Maggie would never cease to amaze him.

He kissed her. He'd only meant to kiss her briefly. He wasn't even sure why. He wanted to, so he did. He could taste the vanilla ice cream. Her lips were incredibly soft beneath his. His only thought was he didn't want to stop kissing her.

Chapter Ten

Brady's lips were pressed against hers, firm and questing. Maggie couldn't help but part hers on a sigh, surrendering to the pent-up passion.

Until her mind butted in with the reminder that this was some other woman's man. In New York, she hadn't known, but now...

She pushed her hands on Brady's chest, breaking the connection. His eyes were hazy and confused.

"What about..." She searched for the name she'd heard today. "Jules?"

His eyebrows drew together. "What about Jules?"

"Wow." Her hands were on his chest and she could feel the muscle beneath her fingertips. Heat flushed her cheeks, remembering how his naked skin felt pressed against hers. She pulled her hands away from the fire that he ignited in her. Crossing her arms to keep them from checking out other muscles, she looked down her nose at him as she tried to rally her indignation. "Your girlfriend?"

Brady had the audacity to appear genuinely confused. "Jules?"

"I'm not stupid." Though she was starting to wonder about him. "I heard you on the phone today. You said you were dating."

Clarity transformed his face into a grin. "Aah."

"Do you typically kiss other women when you date someone these days? Because I can tell you, I'm not okay with that." Maggie wished she'd felt that way the minute his lips touched hers, but they hummed with pleasure and longed to jump right back into kissing.

"I'm not dating Jules." He closed the distance between them.

She backed up a step on the porch stairs. "I'm not a fool. Just because I'm here doesn't mean I'm available."

"Are you involved with someone?" He stepped onto the bottom step, bringing their bodies within touching distance again. Even though the night was cooling rapidly, his heat curled out from his body and wrapped itself around her.

"I'm not a cheater," she said in her best holier-than-thou voice.

His wolfish grin hit her below the belt. His gaze roamed over her possessively. She almost stumbled trying to get up another step.

"Just because your girlfriend isn't here doesn't make you available." She held her chin a little higher, proud that she hadn't crumpled under the power of the attraction between them.

"Jules isn't my girlfriend." He stepped again and they were eye to eye, chest to chest.

"But you said—"

"I said she could tell Peterson, a coworker of ours, that we were dating so that he'd stop asking her out. He won't take no for an answer." He reached out and tucked her hair behind her ear. His hand slipped behind her neck and every nerve in her body tingled in response. "I wouldn't betray her or you in that way, Maggie."

"Oh." Her brain completely shut down on her. The blue of his eyes held her hypnotized, waiting for his next move. Her whole body was a shiver of anticipation.

"Found it!" Amber shouted through the door.

Brady touched his forehead to hers. "To be continued."

Brady sat at the table as Amber leafed through the pages of a scrapbook. Maggie had followed him in and disappeared.

"I wasn't allowed to have a dog, but Nana let me put the stickers on this page, anyway." Amber pointed at the little stickers of dogs surrounding a picture of Amber and Mrs. Brown.

"We have a dog out at the farm. His name is Barnabus." Brady tried to not get distracted wondering where Maggie was and if she'd felt the same powerful draw that he had.

"I've never been on a farm. Is it like the zoo?" Amber turned the page. "See, we went to the zoo. It took a really long time to get there."

"Never been on a farm?" Brady needed to stay focused on Amber.

Amber tucked her dark hair behind her ear. A motion he'd seen Maggie do at least a dozen times. "Billy has a farm, but I'm not friends with him."

"We'll have to fix that." Brady pointed to a picture of Maggie with a monkey. "Did you take this?"

"Yeah, Mommy said it was silly, but I liked the picture." She closed the scrapbook and met his eyes. "Would you take me to your farm?"

"It's not my farm," he said automatically. "My brother runs it, but I grew up there. I'd love to show you around."

"This weekend?" Amber gave him a pleading smile and put her hands together. "Do you have horses?"

"Maybe. We don't have horses."

Amber gazed intently at his eyes. "You have the same color of eyes that I do."

Brady held his breath. Would she make the connection?

"Time for bed, baby," Maggie called from the other room.

"Will I see you tomorrow? Please, please, please, say yes."

"I'll try. I have some work to get done, but I'll be over after. Especially if your mother is cooking." He tweaked her nose with his finger.

Amber giggled and gave him a hug around his shoulders from behind him before running upstairs.

He took in a breath. This was familiar, yet foreign to him. Nights at the Ward farm had always been slow and easy, but nothing about his life since Tawnee Valley had been slow or easy. It was hard to remember how it felt to relax.

"You'll be by tomorrow?" Maggie swept past him to the kitchen sink and started filling it with water.

"Planning on it." He scrubbed his face, suddenly tired. "Can I help?"

"Sure." Her voice was tight.

He took the drying towel and waited while she washed a few dishes. How many nights had he spent with his mother, helping with the dishes? The silence between Maggie and him was comfortable and distracting at the same time. How could he recapture that moment on the porch steps? And if he did, would he have the energy to follow through?

They finished the dinner dishes. She scrubbed the counters while he dried the last dish.

She took the towel from him and hung it before turning out the kitchen light. "You'll think about what I said? About telling Amber?"

"Yes." Brady followed her through the dining room to the

front door where she held it open. Apparently, she didn't want to pick up where they'd left off on the porch steps. Maybe she was as exhausted as he felt.

"She needs to know." Maggie finally met his gaze.

What he wouldn't give to wipe away the weariness from her. To ease her burden.

"I'll tell her. I promise."

"More promises." She half smiled.

"Promises I intend to keep." Brady stepped close, but she retreated when he lifted his hand toward her.

"I don't think that is a good idea." Her face was stern, but there was a breathless quality to her voice that encouraged him.

"Not tonight," Brady said.

"Not ever." Maggie leaned against the wall. "I'm tired, Brady. I can't play this cat-and-mouse game as well as you can. I'm attracted to you."

He didn't move, sensing the "but" behind her words. "I'm attracted to you, too."

"I can't be what makes you go away." Her face flushed and her bottom lip trembled.

"I don't understand…" Why would she worry about that?

"My dad left when I was six." Her face went blank as if she felt nothing, but he could feel the pain underscoring every word. "I thought Mom had driven him away and I hated her for a while. Then I thought it was my fault and I hated myself for it."

"I wouldn't do that to Amber." He started to reach out but she flinched away. "Or you."

"You don't know that. I don't know that." She straightened. "We are much better off as friends. That way this doesn't get confused into something it's not. It never was."

Her smile had a touch of sadness to it. He wanted to reassure her, but he didn't know how much of himself he could give…to Amber or to her. When things had gotten rough in the past, he'd run. How could he guarantee he wouldn't do the same now?

Maybe this was for the best. He nodded. "It never was."

Her smile vanished though she tried to hold on to it. "I'll see you tomorrow."

"Tomorrow." Brady stepped out of the house and the weight of the world crashed down on his shoulders. He had people relying on him in New York and people relying on him in Tawnee Valley. Part of him wanted to run away, hide in his work. But as he settled into his rented car, he glanced up as the porch light turned off. Maggie stood silhouetted in the doorway.

No, this time he'd be the brave one. This time he'd build a relationship with his daughter and make sure that it didn't fall apart when something major happened. He'd be her rock, the way Maggie's father should have been for her. He wouldn't run.

The week turned out to be more hectic than Brady had estimated. Contractors had change orders. Reports had to be in on time. Jules was barely staying afloat.

It was Wednesday and he'd sworn to Maggie and Amber that he'd be by today, but someone above must have a sense of humor, because everything was falling apart at work.

The sun beat on his head as he tried to shield the screen of his laptop. He had his earpiece firmly in and was listening in on a conference Peterson had called.

"We need to increase the budget by at least five hundred thousand dollars to make sure the project doesn't have overages," Peterson said.

"The budget is fine as is and with all the current work orders inputted, we should have a small bit of excess left over in case of another change," Jules said. "An increase is uncalled for. What we have is sufficient."

Brady glanced up at the sound of a truck coming down the old country road. The only place on the farm that received decent reception was at the top of the driveway near the mailbox. Cars rarely came this way, but a lot of farm equipment went past. Of course, if the driver caught a glimpse of Brady, they would stop and chat for at least ten minutes.

The mail truck came around the corner and stopped at the box.

"Brady, didn't your mother ever teach you to wear a hat?" Betsy Griffin tipped her postal cap at him. "You'll get those good looks burnt right off ya."

Brady muted the conference. "If mine gets messed up at least there are two more just like me."

Betsy chuckled and tucked a strand of gray hair up into her cap.

"You tell that brother of yours that his mutt has been up to no good. There are about five puppies on my farm that look an awful lot like that shaggy dog of his."

"I'll let him know."

"You take care now." Betsy tipped her cap and drove off.

Brady and Sam had managed to maintain a good distance from each other. Sam was always out of the house by the time Brady got going in the morning. He couldn't afford to get into it with Sam if he wanted to stay.

He glanced at his screen and unmuted his phone.

"Brady?" Jules's voice sounded concerned.

"I'm here."

"Did we get cut off?"

"No. Someone stopped by. Meeting over?" Brady eyed the time. If he was going to see Amber tonight, he'd need to wrap up quickly.

"Yes."

"What did I miss?"

Jules filled him in on the proposed changes and how she'd fought to keep the budget the same. Peterson had backed down at the end. Brady could almost hear the triumph in her voice.

"If you need anything, text me nine-one-one and I'll call you." Brady closed his laptop and put it in the bag. "Anything at all."

"Spend time with your daughter. I'll see you when you get back to New York." Jules hung up.

Brady stretched as he stood and looked over the old farmhouse and the land surrounding it. The brothers had spent many days working the fields and helping their father make the most out of the land they had. Generations of Wards had worked these fields before them. Now it all fell to Sam.

The house needed a coat of paint, but the barn looked in good repair. Instead of being held together by whatever scraps their father could find, it looked as though Sam had gone through and made the barn a solid structure.

Unlike Sam, who seemed to thrive on the farm, Brady had never belonged here. Even when he had been at the top of his game in high school, he'd felt as if something was missing. He collected the mail and headed down the drive.

Being in England hadn't helped. He hadn't found anywhere that made him feel whole. Like a puzzle with a piece missing, he kept trying to fill it with work and accomplishments, but it didn't seem to help. Each step forward made him want to reach for the next level.

The screen door screeched as he opened it. Inside the house it was cool with the windows open and the lights out. He flung the mail on the kitchen table and started to set his bag on the chair when he caught sight of an envelope with red on it.

FINAL NOTICE. Brady snatched the bill and sank into the kitchen chair.

"Sam?" he yelled.

No one answered. Sam must be down in the field or in the barn. Brady tore open the envelope and stared at the balance. He shifted through the other mail and found a few more overdue bills.

He stormed out the back door and crossed to the barn. Soundgarden's "Fell on Black Days" blasted from the garage in the back. The garage smelled of oil and gasoline, bringing forward the memory of his father, leaning over their old truck's engine while Brady, barely Amber's age, sat on the toolbox ready to hand him a tool, loving every moment of his father's attention.

"What is this?" Brady demanded as he hit the off button on the dirt-coated boom box.

Sam rolled out from under the tractor on the creeper their father had always used. His face was smeared with grease and sweat. He glanced at the notices in Brady's hands. "None of your business."

He rolled back under the tractor.

"I sent money. How did you get behind?" Brady moved around the tractor, trying to see Sam's face.

Sam stayed under the tractor and swiped at his face with an old rag that was too dirty to do any good. His blue coveralls had rips in one knee and were badly in need of a wash. He dropped the wrench and grabbed a screwdriver.

"Dammit, Sam. This is something you need to pay attention to. You can't ignore these and hope they'll go away." The balance on the bill in Brady's hand was a couple of thousand alone. But combined with the others and the ones he didn't know about, it could be a hefty sum. "They could force you to file bankruptcy."

"I'll take care of it," Sam grumbled.

"If you need money, I can help—"

"Money?" Sam rolled out from under the tractor and sat

with his arms resting on his knees. The expression on Sam's face said Brady was being ignorant. "And that will solve everything?"

"In this case…" Brady looked pointedly at the bill. "Yes."

"Do you remember how to work?" Sam pushed to his feet and dropped the screwdriver into a metal tool chest with a loud clang before slamming the drawer shut.

"I work every day—"

"Behind that little computer of yours. Pushing buttons." Sam made little typing motions in the air before he jerked open another drawer and pulled out a socket wrench.

"And I make money doing it. I use my brains and not my brute strength. I create jobs for people." Brady met Sam's gaze. He wasn't going to give in on this. What he did was important. It took a lot of effort to coordinate the projects to make sure everything went smoothly and according to plan.

"And I don't use my brain?" Sam tapped the socket wrench against his hand, lightly.

"It's different and it doesn't change the fact that you are swimming in a sea of debt that this farm can't sustain."

"How would you know?" Sam dropped down on the rolling cart, planting his feet firmly on the concrete floor. "What do you know about farming?"

Brady opened his mouth and closed it. He'd been away for eight years. Though he'd helped Mom balance the bank accounts and been the one to figure out their father's will and hers, he knew nothing about what the finances were now.

"It took Dad, you, me and Luke to keep this farm running on a regular basis during the summer. If the farm had a good year with sufficient rain for the crops and the coyotes didn't get too much of the livestock, we made ends meet." Sam pointed the socket wrench at Brady. "The money you sent helped pay for part of this barn."

"I sent a hell of a lot more money than—"

"And you had a child that needed taking care of."

"If I'd known about my child, I would have taken care of her."

"I didn't need the money." Sam acted as if Brady hadn't said anything. "We were doing fine. Luke was home for the summers for a few years. But then he got busy with med school. I had to pay for someone to come and work *our* farm." Sam cracked his neck. "I fell behind a little. Sue me."

Sam disappeared under the tractor. Brady wasn't ready to push the fact that Sam had kept Amber a secret. Losing the farm was too important. It would have destroyed his parents.

Brady couldn't erase time and return to Tawnee Valley eight years ago and hang around to help out. He couldn't erase what had happened to Maggie, Sam or Amber. All he could do was offer the future.

"Let me look over your books," Brady said.

"What? So you can tell me what I'm doing wrong?" The sound of metal hitting metal emanated through the garage.

"What do you think I've been doing the past eight years?"

"Besides getting soft?"

"Working on budgets and figuring out how to minimize spending and maximize profits." Brady started to lean against the workbench, but when a daddy longlegs shuffled past, he decided against it. "If you won't take my money, at least let me figure out a payment plan, so you can find your way out of this hole without losing the farm."

"I won't lose the farm." Not even a hint of fear in Saint Sam's voice, but there was an underlying tightness. "You weren't the only one with plans. I was at college when Mom got sick, but I gave that up for her, you and Luke. And when Mom died and left Luke to me, I made you go to college, follow your dreams. Figuring you'd find your way home eventually. Guess I was wrong about that."

"I never meant to dump that on you," Brady bit out. He'd

struggled with the guilt, but he'd known he had to go his own way.

"This farm has been in our family for over a century. I won't lose it now." Sam banged something with the wrench. The sound of metal against metal reverberated in the space.

"Just let me look it over." Brady felt as though he was ten trying to convince twelve-year-old Sam to let him have a turn with the basketball.

Sam rolled out and wiped his hands on the dirty rag. "Only if you get off your damn high horse and make yourself useful around here."

"Do you have any idea how much work I have to do?" Brady could feel his face getting redder by the second. Between Maggie's demands and Sam's, he wouldn't be able to get any work done on the Detrex project.

"I'm sure there's someone as fancy as you working up there in New York, getting things done just fine without you." Sam stood and took the bill from Brady's hands. He glanced over it with his usual stoic face.

Fighting with Sam was as fruitless as fighting with Maggie. He'd done them both a disservice and owed them a little of his time in payment. He had left his brother when he needed him most. Sam *had* raised Luke, no matter how much Brady tried to justify that he'd been away at school. He could have gone to a college closer, so he could help whenever needed. But he'd let his pain control him, and New York hadn't been far enough away. He'd had to detach himself so much that he hadn't bothered to keep in touch with anyone from Tawnee Valley except for Luke. Even then, Luke had been the one contacting him, not the other way around.

Maybe he could make up for the time that he'd lost by helping out. He glanced at his watch and wondered what Maggie was doing.

Brady sighed. "Just tell me what needs to be done."

Chapter Eleven

"A no-show, huh?" Penny snatched a carrot from the plate Maggie was setting on the table.

"He said Sam needed his help." Maggie avoided meeting Penny's gaze, afraid she'd catch on to the disappointment Maggie had felt when Brady called an hour ago.

"Want me to beat him up for you?" Penny straddled a chair and held her fists like a boxer. "I could hit him right where it counts."

"That won't be necessary." When Penny sagged in defeat, Maggie added, "Yet."

"What's for dinner?" Amber came in and sat next to Penny.

"Chicken." Maggie hurried to the kitchen. What she wanted to do was go outside and have a good scream, but she needed to keep it together until Penny went home and Amber went to bed. She hoped this didn't become a habit with Brady.

"Is Brady coming over?" Amber called to her.

Maggie took in a deep breath and forced a smile before returning to the dining room with the platter of chicken. "No, honey, he has work to do."

"Can't he do it over here?" Just a hint of a whine had entered Amber's voice.

"Nope."

"What am I, chopped liver?" Penny tickled Amber's side until Amber giggled and batted her hand away.

Amber leaned in close to Penny's ear and said in a loud whisper, "I think Mommy likes Brady."

Penny raised an eyebrow at Maggie, but turned and whispered, "I think Brady likes your Mommy, too."

Amber nodded and giggled.

Maggie could feel the heat rising in her cheeks. "I do not like Brady."

"They looked like they were going to kiss on the porch," Amber told Penny.

Maggie groaned and refused to look at Penny. "Eat your dinner."

She passed around the food until everyone had a full plate. Penny kept trying to catch her eye, which Maggie avoided at all costs. She didn't want to go into details with Penny until Maggie knew how she felt about Brady.

Amber chatted away about school. Maggie forced herself to participate in the conversation. Ever since last night, though, only one thing had occupied her mind—that kiss. It had been one thing to kiss him in New York. Different place, right mood, old lover, that type of thing. But here? On her front porch?

She'd been on edge since she got home from work, waiting. Waiting for Brady to come over and finish what he'd started. Even though she'd told him it would be better if they didn't. Even though she could almost feel every touch, the slide of his skin against hers, his mouth against hers and traveling

HARLEQUIN® READER SERVICE—Here's How It Works:

Accepting your 2 free books and 2 free gifts (gifts valued at approximately $10.00) places you under no obligation to buy anything. You may keep the books and gifts and return the shipping statement marked "cancel". If you do not cancel, about a month later we'll send you 6 additional books and bill you just $4.74 each in the U.S. or $5.24 each in Canada. That's a savings of at least 14% off the cover price. It's quite a bargain! Shipping and handling is just 50¢ per book in the U.S. and 75¢ per book in Canada.* You may cancel at any time, but if you choose to continue, every month we'll send you 6 more books, which you may either purchase at the discount price or return to us and cancel your subscription.

*Terms and prices subject to change without notice. Prices do not include applicable taxes. Sales tax applicable in N.Y. Canadian residents will be charged applicable taxes. Offer not valid in Quebec. All orders subject to credit approval. Credit or debit balances in a customer's account(s) may be offset by any other outstanding balance owed by or to the customer. Please allow 4 to 6 weeks for delivery. Offer available while quantities last.

If offer card is missing write to: Harlequin Reader Service, P.O. Box 1867, Buffalo NY 14240-1867 or visit www.ReaderService.com

HSE-L7-05/13

NO POSTAGE
NECESSARY
IF MAILED
IN THE
UNITED STATES

BUSINESS REPLY MAIL
FIRST-CLASS MAIL   PERMIT NO. 717   BUFFALO, NY

POSTAGE WILL BE PAID BY ADDRESSEE

HARLEQUIN READER SERVICE

PO BOX 1867

BUFFALO NY 14240-9952

GET FREE BOOKS and FREE GIFTS
WHEN YOU PLAY THE...

Just scratch off the silver box with a coin. Then check below to see the gifts you get!

SLOT MACHINE GAME!

YES!
I have scratched off the silver box. Please send me the 2 free Harlequin® Special Edition® books and 2 free gifts for which I qualify. I understand I am under no obligation to purchase any books, as explained on the back of this card.

235/335 HDL FV7W

FIRST NAME	LAST NAME

ADDRESS

APT.#	CITY

STATE/PROV.	ZIP/POSTAL CODE

7 7 7	**Worth TWO FREE BOOKS plus 2 FREE Mystery Gifts!**
🍒 🍒 🍒	**Worth TWO FREE BOOKS!**
♣ ♣ ♣	**Worth ONE FREE BOOK!**
🔔 🔔 🔔	**TRY AGAIN!**

Visit us at: www.ReaderService.com

HSE-L7-05/13

DETACH AND MAIL CARD TODAY!

Printed in the U.S.A. ® and ™ are trademarks owned and used by the trademark owner and/or its licensee. © 2012 HARLEQUIN ENTERPRISES LIMITED lower. God, how she'd wanted him and what she wouldn't give to feel that way. Complete abandon.

Which would be a mistake. Huge mistake.

"Earth to Maggie." Penny waved her hand in front of Maggie's face.

Maggie snapped to attention. "What?"

"Amber asked you a question." Penny gave her an expectant look.

"I'm sorry, baby." Maggie shook off the lingering images from her past. "What was your question?"

"Why don't you ask Brady out on a date? Penny would watch me, wouldn't you?" Amber's blue eyes were huge and innocent and hopeful.

Maggie snapped her gaze to Penny to see if she had put Amber up to this, but Penny held up her hands as if to say, "Don't look at me." She sighed and turned to Amber.

"It isn't that easy." Maggie tried to think of excuses and reasons and anything but Brady's hand on the back of her neck. An involuntary shudder raced along her spine.

"Why not?"

"Yeah, Maggie, why not?" Penny leaned her elbows on the table and added her questioning look to Amber's.

"Because…" Oh, hell, what was she supposed to say? That she didn't like him? Then the question would be why he was hanging around. Until Brady was ready to come forward to Amber about being her father, her hands were tied.

"Go on." Penny was enjoying this way too much.

If things were different, she might have jumped at the chance to ask Brady out. "He lives in New York and we live in Tawnee Valley. It would never work out. Besides, we're just friends."

She took her dishes to the kitchen. Logically, that was true. Brady didn't have a burning desire to move back to Tawnee

Valley anytime soon. In fact, it seemed he couldn't wait to get away from it.

She turned to find both Amber and Penny looking at her from the doorway.

"What now?" she said.

"I like Brady," Amber said. Plain and simple as if that were the cure-all to the world.

Sensing a trap, Maggie hesitated before saying, "I like him, too."

Penny covered her mouth to hide her chuckle. Maggie glared at her, but she waited patiently for Amber to get out what she wanted to say.

"You should date." Amber disappeared into the dining room. The clatter of dishes being stacked filled the room.

"Did you put her up to this?" Maggie whispered and pointed toward the dining room.

"No, but the look on your face is priceless." Penny's grin infuriated Maggie more.

Amber reappeared with the dishes and took them to the sink. "Are you waiting for my father to come back?"

Maggie's mouth dropped open and she honestly couldn't think of a single thing to say. Even if Amber knew Brady was her father, she would probably be wondering the same thing. Maggie hadn't dated because the available men in Tawnee Valley greatly dwindled after high school age. And the ones that were available weren't what she wanted.

Penny gave her a phony serious look. "Yeah, Maggie. What are you waiting for?"

Maggie narrowed her eyes at Penny before squatting in front of Amber. "What's bringing all of this up now?"

Amber scrunched her face as if she were trying to keep the truth from coming out, before bursting out with, "Jessica said that her mom thinks you should get back with Brady."

Maggie closed her eyes. Damned if she does, damned if

she doesn't. What was she going to say to that? That she and Brady had never really been together? Then when Amber found out about Brady being her father, Maggie would have to explain that sometimes people don't have to love each other to have a child.

"Do you love Brady, Mommy?"

That one struck her right in the heart.

"You know what, runt?" Penny said and held out her hand to Amber. "Maybe we should lay off Mommy for a little while. Let's go find that book we were reading the other night."

Maggie mouthed "Thank you" to Penny as Penny led Amber out of the kitchen. Already almost on the floor, she dropped on the old linoleum and sagged against the dark oak cabinets.

Did she love Brady? In high school, she believed she was in love with him, but how could you love someone who barely acknowledged your existence? Okay, she had loved him in that first-crush, puppy-love kind of way, completely unrequited.

But now…he'd changed so much that he didn't seem like the same guy. She saw hints of the guy she'd crushed on in high school, but that wasn't the only thing that drew her. When they'd walked the streets in New York surrounded by people, she'd been the only one that had mattered to him. Or when he maneuvered them though the airport, always careful to make sure she didn't fall behind or get lost. Or when he touched her face to wipe away the tear when she'd confessed about her own father.

To say that she had a crush on Brady was putting it mildly. The way he was with Amber when he was in the moment and focused was amazing. He'd even caved to her request about work. Even if he missed coming over, he'd respected her wishes.

"You okay?" Penny stepped into the kitchen and slid down the cabinets to sit next to Maggie.

"I don't know."

"You know I love to tease you, right?" Penny bumped her shoulder against Maggie's.

"Yeah." Maggie leaned her head against the cabinet and rolled it until she faced Penny. "What am I going to do?"

"First, you are going to thank me for distracting your daughter."

"Thank you." Maggie reached out and took Penny's hand. "Really. Thank you for being here for me. You don't know how much I rely on you."

"What are best friends for?" Penny shrugged but squeezed Maggie's hand. "As for Brady…"

"Yeah. Brady." Maggie thudded her head against the cabinets.

"You've got a great daughter, Maggie. And maybe Brady won't be that bad of a dad for her, but you have to look at the big picture."

"What's the big picture?" Maggie desperately wanted to know.

Penny clasped her hands around Maggie's. "Amber is putting this together faster than either of you expected. Brady needs to come clean and you need to figure out what type of relationship you are going to have with each other and with Amber."

"I already told him that I didn't want to get involved with him because of Amber."

"Why not?"

Maggie struggled to find words, but finally pulled it together. "Because—"

"Brady isn't your dad. He's not going to leave Amber. At his worst, Brady's a workaholic. He earns good money and has kept fit unlike most of the men around here. You could do a lot worse than Brady Ward."

"But—"

"Don't give me the whole New York-versus-here thing. What are you really worried about?"

Maggie took a deep, shaky breath. "That the only reason he wants me is because he loves Amber."

Brady pocketed his phone as he got out of the car. He'd made sure to set the ringer to vibrate in case Jules needed to reach him. All day they'd worked with a contractor who was refusing to listen to anyone but Brady, which was frustrating for both Jules and him. Something he hoped Peterson didn't get wind about.

When Brady hadn't been on the phone or the computer, Sam had kept him busy working the farm.

He wasn't about to let another day go by where he didn't see Amber, though. A sharp high-pitched bark met him as he opened the rear car door.

"Are you ready?" Brady said to the puppy in the cardboard box.

The puppy wagged his tail and barked in response. Brady hooked on the leash to the new collar he'd bought and set the puppy on the ground. Barnabus, Sam's dog, was a pretty big dog and this "puppy" was going to be large like his daddy. He was already the size of a small dog.

Maybe Brady should have checked with Maggie before bringing the gift, but he remembered Amber saying that she'd always wanted one. When Sam had begrudgingly brought home a couple of the pups to pawn off to other people, he'd happily given one to Brady.

The puppy took off toward the house with Brady in tow. Brady knocked on the side of the screen door.

"Just a second." Maggie. The sound of her voice rushed through him.

He tried to stop the direction his thoughts were headed, but when Maggie appeared at the door with her hair wet in a pair of cut-offs and a green T-shirt that made the green in her hazel eyes stand out, his brain stopped altogether.

"Hey, Brady, Amber's bus gets here in about ten minutes." She met his eyes and smiled.

The puppy whined and her smile faded as her eyes dropped to see the white fuzz ball. "You brought a dog?"

"He's a puppy." Brady's brain was occupied with mentally peeling off every layer of her clothing and imagining what they could do in ten minutes.

"*That* is a puppy?"

His gaze lingered a moment longer at her breasts before finally arriving at her not-pleased-at-all face. His brain shifted into gear. Definitely should have checked. "Yeah. Sam's dog got out in the spring and this little guy is the end result."

"There is nothing little about that puppy." Her eyes rounded in horror. "Please don't tell me you brought that for Amber."

"Why? She was saying how much she wanted a dog the other day and how she couldn't have one…" Realization settled in his stomach like a lump of Sam's burned eggs. "And you were the one who didn't want a dog, right?"

"Do you know how much work a dog is? Let alone a puppy?"

He hated hearing the disappointment in her voice. Hated it even more because he was the one she was disappointed with. "I can say he's come for a visit?"

She narrowed her eyes and crossed her arms. "You know the minute she sees that fur ball she's going to love it."

"I guess he doesn't have that effect on you?" Brady said curtly.

"Who do you think gets stuck with the feeding and cleaning and taking him out at three in the morning in the snow? Not to mention housetraining."

"Like I said—"

"You got me a dog!" Amber's squeal of delight was met by little excited puppy barks.

Maggie gave him the see-I-told-you look. But Amber's eyes glowed with happiness as she shrugged off her backpack and knelt before the puppy. When the puppy proceeded to bathe her face with his tongue, her giggles made Brady feel as if he'd brought her the moon and not a mutt.

"You are such a licker. I'll name you Flicker," Amber proclaimed. "Licker would be weird."

Brady cleared his throat to get Amber's attention. "I brought him for a visit."

Her fingers tightened into the puppy's fur and her face fell with disappointment. His heart tightened. He almost said she could keep the dog, but Maggie had already made it clear she didn't want it.

"But I'll see if Sam wants to keep him out at the farm, so you can visit Flicker." Brady knew Sam hadn't been pleased with the idea of more dogs, but in the grand scheme of things, Sam owed Brady more than Brady owed Sam. At least, Brady wanted to think that, but looking at the girl nuzzling this fur ball, he wondered what Sam had given up to take care of Mom, Luke and him.

"Do you have homework?" Maggie opened the screen door. Flicker immediately burst into the house, causing Maggie to scowl at Brady.

"I'll get him." Brady brushed past her. His side pressed against hers for the briefest moment, but it sent electricity coursing through his veins.

Amber was hot on his heels. He managed to grab the leash before Flicker got to the trash can.

"Can we take him for a walk?" Amber looked to her

mother for approval. "I've always wanted to do that. Can
we? Please?"

"The dog can stay for dinner, but he has to go home with
Brady." Maggie crossed her arms over her chest and met
Brady's gaze. "You are responsible for any damage that dog
does."

Obviously, Brady wasn't the only one Amber could wrap
around her finger. "That's fine."

"The walk, Mom?" Amber struck a similar pose to her
mother.

"Go ahead, but then it's straight to homework. And Brady
has to go with you."

Amber raced to the front door. The puppy followed on her
heels, jumping on her when she stopped.

Maggie grabbed his arm as he passed. When he stopped,
she pulled her hand away as if he were burning her. Maybe
he had because his skin felt singed from her touch.

"He's too big for her to handle," she said.

"We'll be fine, Maggie." He resisted the urge to kiss her
scowl away and pulled on Flicker's leash.

The screen door slammed behind them as Flicker and
Amber raced down the stairs. The puppy kept trying to grab
the end of Amber's shirt, but she kept it away from him with
a little shriek of joy.

Brady jerked on the leash and the puppy came rushing
to him. "Maybe if we walk together, Flicker will learn his
manners."

"Okay." Amber fell into step with Brady. The warmth of
the day had settled with a gentle breeze. The puppy darted
from tree to tree and jerked slightly on Brady's hold.

"Are you dating anyone?" Amber walked beside him.

"No."

"Have you had many girlfriends?"

Brady wasn't used to anyone being so direct with him, but

he found Amber refreshing. He already had one lie he had to come clean on. He figured the least he could do was honestly answer her questions. "A few."

"Did you have any girlfriends in London?" Amber watched the puppy as he burrowed underneath some leaves.

"I had a few dates, but no one I'd call a girlfriend." Brady pulled on the leash as Flicker tried to veer off into someone's yard.

"Why not? Don't you like girls?" Amber stopped and cocked her head to the side.

Brady stopped his mouth from gaping. "I do but I didn't have time because of work."

Amber nodded as if she understood completely. He couldn't help but wonder if she did. He had no idea what a seven-year-old thought about or even knew. Apparently, more than he thought.

"Is New York big?" Amber asked.

"Millions of people live there." Brady felt his phone vibrate in his pocket, notifying him of a text.

"How did Mom find you in all those people?"

Brady looped the leash around his wrist and grabbed his phone. Now that they'd settled into a slower pace, Flicker walked beautifully as if he'd been raised on a leash. "The same way you find anyone. She had an address and a phone number."

He flipped on the screen and saw the text from Jules. Nine-one-one. Crap.

"Amber?" Brady stopped. Flicker came bounding back to see what the holdup was.

"Yes?" She had squatted next to Flicker and petted him to keep him calm.

"Do you think you could take the leash for a few minutes? I need to make a quick phone call."

"You want me to walk Flicker?" Amber held out her hands and bounced slightly in place.

Brady glanced at the dog who had decided to chew on his own leg. Flicker hadn't tugged on the leash recently and seemed fairly calm. Amber could handle the puppy. He handed the leash to her. "Wrap it around your wrist and be careful not to let go, otherwise, we'll have to chase Flicker."

"I promise." Amber wrapped the leash around her wrist. "Come on, Flicker."

They all started forward again as Brady called Jules. "Hey, Jules, I can't talk long. What's going on?"

"The contractor wants to charge us double for the most recent change order. I tried to reason with him, but he says that you and he had a deal." Jules sounded exhausted.

Brady stopped, but Amber kept going. "Jules, tell him that you are in charge and you know every deal that I've made. If he's not going to work with you, we'll have to find someone else."

"Flicker, no!"

Brady's heart stopped as he looked up. Amber was tangled in Flicker's leash. Before Brady could even move, Flicker jerked on the leash, and Amber crashed to the sidewalk, landing in a heap. Flicker bounded to Amber's side as Brady rushed to her.

Amber's cries filled the air and made Brady's heart ache, even as his pulse raced. Flicker whimpered and started licking the back of Amber's head.

"Are you okay?" Brady knelt on the ground and pulled the leash away from Amber's legs. He shoved Flicker's nose away from Amber's face as he helped her into a sitting position.

Her dirt-smudged face didn't seem to have any cuts on it. Her tears tore at something deep inside him. He should have caught her. That's what daddies did.

She held up her bleeding hands that she must have used to stop her fall. "My knee."

Her knee was a mess of blood and dirt.

Her eyes welled with more tears. Her cries changed into soft sobs. "I didn't know Flicker would pull. Don't tell Mommy. She'll blame Flicker."

"No, she won't." Brady slipped his arms under her and lifted her from the ground. He grabbed the leash. Maggie wouldn't blame Flicker for Amber getting hurt.

No, Maggie would blame Brady.

Chapter Twelve

Maggie finished slicing the potatoes for dinner, trying to keep her anger inside. He brought a puppy to her house. He chose work over Amber, but he thought he could buy them with a puppy. Footsteps stomped up the porch and the screen door banged.

"Maggie?" Brady called out with a tinge of worry in his voice.

"Mommy." Amber's voice was shaky and tear-filled.

Maggie had heard that tone enough to know Amber was hurt. Grabbing a kitchen towel, she dried her hands as she rushed to the entryway.

Brady stood there, cradling Amber to his chest. In one hand was the puppy's leash and in the other, his blasted cell phone. She glared at him for a split second before checking over Amber. Scraped hands and knees.

"All right, let's take this circus act to the bathroom," Maggie said calmly. Her stomach wouldn't settle until she had a

chance to make sure nothing was broken, but being hysteri-
cal wouldn't help anyone.

She reached into the medicine cabinet and got out the
cleanser and antibacterial cream along with the Band-Aids.
The bathroom was small on a normal day but with Brady
holding Amber and a rambunctious puppy bounding all
around, her nerves were on end.

"Put her down on the toilet."

"She's going to be fine. I had all sorts of cuts and scrapes
growing up." Brady sounded as if he was trying to reassure
himself more than anyone else.

Maggie handed him paper towels. "Wet these. We need to
clean the wound to see what type of damage has been done."

"Of course." Taking the paper towels, he went to the sink.
He seemed startled to find the phone in his hand. Setting it
on the edge of the sink, he turned on the water.

Maggie squatted before Amber. Amber's tears had started
to dry, but she sniffled slightly. The puppy sat in the corner
near the tub and started whining.

"What hurts?"

"My hands and my knee." Amber glanced over at Brady
before returning her gaze to Maggie. "It's not Flicker's fault,
Mommy. I was messing around."

Right. Maggie pressed her lips together. "Why don't we
get you cleaned up?"

She had a feeling the fault lay with that phone, but she
wouldn't know until she had a chance to talk to Brady. Brady
came over with the wet towels and she moved out of the way.

He knelt beside Amber and gently stroked the wet paper
towel over her knee. Amber winced, biting her lip.

"When I was six, I was helping Dad out in the barn." Brady
moved to one of her hands. "There was an old stool out there
that I liked to stand on."

As Maggie stood, she took Brady's phone. He was so engrossed in helping Amber that he didn't notice. On the screen, it showed he was still connected with Jules. She cut off the call and slipped the phone in her pocket.

"Dad needed this special wrench from above his work-bench." Brady wiped delicately with the paper towel.

As he cleaned off the blood, Maggie could see that the fall had taken off some skin. Amber leaned forward to watch Brady. Her hair fell forward along her cheekbone. She seemed so fragile right now, even though Maggie had patched up worse in the past.

"I climbed on this stool and onto the workbench to get this special wrench." Brady continued his story.

Just as enthralled with his story as Amber, Maggie handed him some cotton soaked with the cleanser.

"When I went to get off the workbench, one of the stool's legs broke and I hit my head on the edge of the old, greasy workbench." Brady held out his hand for the antibacterial and Band-Aids.

"Did it hurt?" Amber asked.

"Bunches." Brady quickly applied the bandages. "I had to go to the hospital and get stitches and shots and everything. I still have a scar."

He touched a spot above his eyebrow and even Maggie leaned forward to see.

"You had to get shots?" Amber's voice was a combination of horror and admiration as she examined the scar. She reached out and traced the small, white line.

Brady nodded. "But you won't need shots. All done. A little battered and bruised but no worse for wear."

He held out a tissue. Amber blew her nose.

"Will you help me with my homework?" Amber gave him her best I'm-hurt smile. "And maybe we can finish our walk with Flicker?"

She avoided looking at Maggie.

"If your mom says it's okay." He looked at Maggie then.

Maggie got caught in his blue eyes. Creases of worry had formed on his forehead and around his eyes. He did care about Amber, even if work had distracted him.

"Sure, that sounds good." Maggie watched both of their faces light up and felt warm and cold at the same time. Amber and Brady loved each other already. She could almost believe that he would always be there for Amber. That they would have each other for the rest of their lives. That Brady wouldn't get tired of being a dad and walk away.

He wasn't like her dad. She had to get that in her mind. But he did live in New York and would eventually leave both of them behind. She could only hope he would be good about staying in touch with Amber after he left.

As she watched them settle at the dining room table with the dog at their feet, chewing on a freshly unwrapped rawhide bone, Maggie couldn't help feeling as though she was on the outside looking in.

"I'm going to go finish dinner." She excused herself, but she could hear the two of them talking in the dining room. It felt right, as if this was how things were meant to be. That they could be a family. Which was ridiculous. Just because he seemed to care for Amber, didn't mean that he wanted to be anything more with her. And even if he did, it wasn't possible with his job and her life here. He would never leave New York.

It all came down to work with him. Brady had obviously taken a work call. During which, Amber must have fallen. Amber's laughter pulled her attention back to the moment. Maggie could hear the low rumble of Brady's voice, but not what he was saying. Amber hadn't said anything about Brady's involvement. Was she protecting him?

They had a little over a week left before Brady returned to New York. When he did, their life would go on as it had before, except Amber would know her father was out there.

What if Brady wanted Amber to go to New York with him? For a few weeks in the summer? Was Maggie ready for that?

She didn't want him to walk out of their lives, but what would his involvement in their lives entail? Would Brady pop in and out of their lives whenever it was convenient for him? Would he be here for Christmas and Thanksgiving and Easter? Birthdays?

"I'm really sorry, Maggie."

She set down the cutting knife and turned to face him. He had stopped in the doorway and leaned his shoulder against the jamb.

"What happened?" She didn't raise her voice. It even came out without sounding accusatory. For emphasis, Maggie crossed her arms and gave him the look she gave Amber to make her confess the bad deed she'd just committed.

"She got tangled in the leash." He almost seemed boyish, looking at her with his head dipped, avoiding saying what would get him in the most trouble. Hoping she'd take whatever explanation he gave. He even dared to give her that sheepish smile that had turned her into mush in high school. Too bad for him it wasn't high school anymore.

"And?" Maggie tried not to tap her foot.

He sighed. "I let Amber hold the leash."

"By herself?"

"Flicker was doing great." The tips of Brady's ears burned red, and she guessed there was more to the story.

"You let her handle an animal that weighs as much as she does?" Maggie couldn't keep her hands from flying as she spoke. "Did you think about what would happen if the dog ran out in the street?"

"But he didn't." Brady's face lost its placating look as he went on the defense.

"And where were you?" She stepped closer and poked him

in the chest. "Where was the great Brady Ward to the rescue? If your hands were free, you could have easily caught her before she hit the ground."

"On an important phone call." He straightened from his leaning position. In high school she would have backed down immediately, but now she didn't feel an ounce of intimidation.

"More important than watching Amber?" The fear when they'd come in had merged with her anger at Brady for bringing the dog in the first place until all she could see was red. "You can't apologize and think that makes it okay. We talked about this. No work when you are with Amber. What part of that didn't you understand?"

"The part where I have to sacrifice everything because of something my brother did." Brady's eyes flashed. She should have retreated, but she couldn't. "Work isn't just money to me. It's my life. It's all I have."

"Not anymore." She poked him in the chest with each syllable for emphasis.

"Do you think I don't know that? That I sleep well at night? That I don't think of a million ways to make this work out best for everyone? News flash. I'm not Superman."

"And who asked you to be? I didn't go to New York to drag your ass back here. I thought you needed to know. You were the one who volunteered to come. You insisted you needed to know her."

He captured her hand against his chest before she could poke him again. "You were the one who insisted now or never. Were you hoping I'd say never?"

She sputtered, "No, of course not."

"You didn't feel at all threatened by the fact that Amber is as much mine as she is yours?" The words were softly spoken but hit her hard in the gut.

His hand held her close to him. The air around them was

thick with tension. What was she supposed to say? Yes, she'd gotten used to having Amber all to herself. Would she deny her daughter her father just to keep things the way they were, which was way more comfortable than how she felt right now with Brady so close?

She should back down, but this was too important. "So why don't you go in there and tell her? Fess up. Stop being such a coward."

"And how do you propose I do that? Just come out and say it? Or should I be like you and wait until she's comfortable before striking?" he said.

"I didn't know you didn't know. Sam—"

"Sending a letter wasn't the only way to reach me and you know it." Brady's blue eyes burned. His breath was hot on her face. "You could have tried other ways."

She pressed her lips together and tilted her chin. Refusing to let him inside her head. To make her doubt her decisions all those years ago. Those questions she'd had when Sam had dropped off the money with no note from Brady. As she examined it over the years, she would wonder, but the older Amber got, the harder it was to admit maybe she'd made a mistake in trusting Sam.

"Admit it, Maggie. You were afraid I'd want something to do with Amber. That I would want to be her father."

Somewhere deep inside she found the strength to step away from Brady. She wasn't backing down, just getting breathing room.

"Why would I be afraid of that?"

He narrowed his eyes. "It doesn't matter. I'm Amber's father and that isn't going to change."

"You're my dad?" Amber's voice sent chills through Maggie's body.

They both turned in time to see the hurt in Amber's eyes before she spun around and ran out the front door.

* * *

Brady cursed. This wasn't the way he had wanted Amber to find out.

Maggie was already at the front door, ready to go after her. Brady reached her in three strides.

"I'll go," he said.

"You don't even know where to look."

Flicker bounced between the two of them obviously excited to be going back outside. Brady grabbed his leash.

"Fine. We'll go together. Where would she go?" Brady opened the door and let Maggie go first.

"I saw her go right before she disappeared behind the bushes. There's the park, the school playground, Amber's friend Mary's house, Penny's. There are a million places she could have gone to." Frustration tinged her voice.

He linked his fingers with hers. "We'll find her."

Her chest rose and fell as she took a deep breath. Her fingers remained entwined with his.

Before they left, the phone rang. Amber had shown up at Penny's. Brady's heart started again, grateful for once that Tawnee Valley was a small town. Maggie squeezed his hand.

When they arrived, Penny simply held open the door. "She's in the living room."

As Penny took the leash from Brady's hand and led Flicker away, Brady followed Maggie into the living room. The yellow walls peeked out in the spaces between the framed pictures on the wall. There were some from high school, some from when Amber was a baby and even some from now. On the blue sofa, Amber sat with a mug of milk and a plate with a few cookies.

"Amber Marie, you can't run out the door like that." Maggie looked as though she was going to scold her more, but Brady tugged her hand. She turned to look at him. In her hazel eyes, the relief over finding Amber only barely covered the fear that had been there before.

"I've got this one." Brady squeezed her hand one more time before letting go. He sat in the floral chair facing the couch.

Amber hadn't made eye contact with either of them. She continued to dunk and eat her cookies as if they weren't there.

Brady struggled to find the words that would put this to right. "We didn't mean for you to find out like that."

Maggie moved behind his chair. Her presence offered him the comfort and support to continue.

How could he make this right?

"I should have let your mom tell you right away, but I was afraid." Brady waited for some indication that she was even listening.

She set the cookie on her plate and lifted her blue eyes. "What were you afraid of?"

"Everything." Brady took a deep breath.

"That's silly." Amber grabbed a napkin and wiped the chocolate from her lips. "How can you be afraid of everything? Are you afraid of cookies?"

"I wish this were simple, but I didn't know about you until your mom came to New York. And then all I wanted to do was meet you, but I thought you wouldn't like me." Brady scrubbed his face with his hand.

"Why wouldn't I like you?"

When she put it so simply, Brady was stumped. "I don't know."

"You're my dad?" Amber was keeping her face blank.

Maggie slid her hand over his shoulder. He was amazed that the touch of her hand could make him feel more in control.

"Yes." Brady waited as Amber thought about it.

"You and Mom were married?"

"No." Brady shifted on the seat. This wasn't headed in a

pleasant direction, but being honest had always served him well in the past. He just wasn't sure that Amber was old enough to understand what had happened between Maggie and Brady when they were young.

Amber sat back in the couch and pulled her feet under her. "But you guys dated? I thought you said you hadn't dated Brady, Mom?"

Maggie's fingers curled into his shoulder. "We knew each other in high school. We were friends."

Friends? They'd barely spoken in high school. They'd had one passionate night. Amber had been the result of that. He needed to get Amber off this path.

"I'm sorry I didn't tell you right away. I should have." Brady leaned forward. Maggie's hand slipped from his shoulder. He met Amber's intense gaze. "Do you forgive me?"

Amber looked from Maggie to Brady and back again. Her nose wrinkled. "Are you going back to New York?"

"In a week." Brady could feel the clamp on his stomach as he waited for her to come to her decision.

"Are you coming back?"

He could almost see the wheels turning in her head. "If you want me to."

She scooted to the edge of her seat. "Am I going to go to New York?"

"I'd love to have you come stay with me." Brady could feel the clamp loosen.

"Can Mom come, too?" Amber spared a glance at her mother.

"We haven't worked out all those details yet," Maggie interrupted.

No, they hadn't. It was probably time they started to think about the future, but not tonight.

"Can I keep Flicker?" Amber had a devious glint in her eyes.

"Is that the only way you'll forgive me?" Brady bit back his smile. Negotiations were supposed to be serious.

"You know the rules, Amber Marie."

Brady wasn't used to Maggie's "mother" voice. It was amazing how much she'd changed in the years since he'd known her.

Amber crumpled her forehead and pouted. "No pets as long as my room looks like a tornado hit it. And I learn some responsi-bil-ity."

"I'm sorry about keeping this from you." Brady was eager to hear her words of forgiveness.

"Do I still call you Brady? Or should I call you Dad or Daddy?" Amber cocked an eyebrow, mimicking her mother perfectly.

"You can call me anything you want." Brady's heart stuttered and filled his chest.

"Dad." Amber tested out the word. "Daddy. Brady."

Flicker barked somewhere in the background.

Amber stood and rounded the coffee table until she stood in front of Brady. They were eye to eye. Brady held his breath. His emotions too overwhelming to pick apart.

"I forgive you and like you just fine, Daddy." Amber's arms closed around Brady's neck.

Brady returned Amber's hug, feeling like the luckiest man alive.

Chapter Thirteen

Brady walked out into the night after helping put Amber to bed. His feet felt glued with each step. Thankfully, Penny had decided to keep Flicker.

What Brady needed was some time alone to think about what being someone's daddy really meant. Did that mean seeing her for two weeks in the summer? Or trying to figure out how to watch a child during an entire semester of schooling in New York? Or spending the holidays in Tawnee Valley with Amber?

And Maggie.

He slid into his rental car and glanced at the two-story Victorian house. How many times had he driven down this street when he was young and never thought anything of this house? Now it housed one of the most important people in Brady's life. His daughter.

His career had always come first, but he could make room in his life for Amber.

Work… He checked his pockets for his phone, but came

up empty-handed. He'd been on it with Jules when Amber got hurt. Damn, he'd forgotten about Jules on the phone.

But what did he do with his phone? He must have left it inside somewhere. He pushed open the door and trudged back to the front door of Maggie's house. Knocking softly so he wouldn't wake Amber, he peeked in the window and saw Maggie crossing the kitchen. She probably couldn't even hear him knocking.

He checked the door and found it unlocked.

"Maggie?" he said softly as he walked in.

It had taken both of them to get Amber to bed. Only Brady promising that he was leaving right away and coming back tomorrow had finally convinced her to go to sleep. He didn't want to risk waking her. Besides, Maggie had seemed as worn-out as he felt.

He crossed the threshold into the kitchen and found Maggie sitting at the table with her head in her hands. He froze at the sight of her.

Her hair fell like silk around her face, softening her and making her seem ageless. Her eyes were closed and her fingers were massaging her temples in slow, steady circles. His fingers flexed and his heart sped. The heaviness lifted slightly.

She'd given him a daughter. A beautiful, intelligent daughter that she'd had to raise on her own because of Sam. He should have been here the entire time. Amber shouldn't have had to learn about him like this, to wonder all this time if her father loved her.

"Maggie?" he said softly.

The chair scraped against the linoleum as she scrambled to face whoever was in the room. Her wide eyes connected with his and realizing it was him, she relaxed.

"Brady? I thought you'd left." She grabbed a towel from the sink. Always busy cleaning something.

"I did, but I think I left my phone. I wanted to let you know before I started searching."

She'd dropped her gaze from his almost immediately. She glanced at him quickly before turning away. Maybe she was still angry about what had happened with Amber.

"I meant what I said earlier." He stepped into the room and walked over to where she stood wiping the counter in a circular motion. He settled his hand on hers. She jerked her hand away, dropping the towel.

"I know you're angry with me, but I don't know what I'm doing anymore." He draped the towel over the bar and finally met her gaze. Instead of anger in her hazel eyes, he saw vulnerability and wariness. It made him stop in his tracks. Did she fear him?

She cleared her throat. Her eyes hid her feelings from him once again. "It's late, Brady."

"You know I'd never do anything intentional to hurt Amber?"

"Of course." But there was a hint of skepticism behind her agreement. She moved to the other side of the kitchen and grabbed the broom.

He closed in on her one step at a time. "There isn't anything I wouldn't do to keep her from feeling the pain you felt as a child, Maggie."

Her lips set firmly together and her chin got that stubborn tilt. It made him want to kiss her until she softened beneath his touch. He stood there, debating whether to close the distance between them or retreat. The emotional roller coaster of the past few hours had him warring with himself. She'd clearly stated that she wanted to keep things as friends between them. But when she was this close, his fingers itched to bury themselves in her hair. His gut tightened and his pulse pounded every time she was in the room.

The few tastes he'd had of her hadn't been enough. He

wanted to feel the curves of her body and explore all those
hidden spots that would make her sigh with pleasure. He
wanted to nibble along her jawline until the hardness left her
face and she sighed his name.

He closed the distance between them. No longer thinking of the consequences. His thumb traced her jawline and
her lips parted. Their eyes were locked, but neither of them
said a word. All he had to do was lean down and kiss her. He
knew she felt it, too.

The noise of the vibration of his phone filtered through
the haze his thoughts had left him in. Maggie jumped as if
something had bitten her. The broom clattered to the floor.
Her head bumped against his chin and he instinctively moved
back.

The buzzing continued. Brady looked around the kitchen
trying to pinpoint the source until his gaze returned to Maggie's red cheeks and downturned face.

"Is that your phone?" Brady stood within touching distance of her and much as he wanted to touch her, he felt as if
he was missing something important.

She shook her head, but finally lifted her eyes to meet his
and that stubborn jaw was set again. Her blush deepened, but
she didn't drop her gaze.

"Is that *my* phone?" Brady asked.

Maggie drew in a breath. "Yes."

He waited, expecting her to do something. Either return
it or explain herself. But she just stood there, defiant and
beautiful.

"May I have it?"

"I'll give it back if you tell me you can separate your work
life and your home life."

"I don't have a home life." Brady ran his hand over his hair.

"You do now." She shoved away from the wall and brushed
past him.

His gaze caught the lump of his phone in her back pocket, but that wasn't what caused his heart to send blood rushing through his body. Her jeans hugged her hips and accented her bottom nicely. He had every intention of getting his hands on those hips again.

She spun around and he barely had the sense to pull his gaze to her eyes. She narrowed her eyes on him. "You have Amber. What's it going to take before you realize that work is only a distraction to what life is really about? Does Amber have to get hit by a car because of your inattention? What if she comes to stay with you in New York? Who's going to watch her while you work? What's the point of her even going if all you are going to do is work? One weekend morning isn't going to be sufficient time to spend with her."

"Fine. I'll leave work at work."

Maggie pulled the phone out of her back pocket and held it out to him. "How can I be sure of that? You already broke that promise to me once."

"I'll leave it at Sam's tomorrow." He closed his hand over the phone, but didn't let go of her hand. "You can't tell me you haven't made any mistakes, Maggie."

"Of course I've made mistakes." Maggie threw her free hand in the air. "But I've learned from them."

She stared pointedly at her hand engulfed by his.

"I see." He released her hand and shoved the phone in his pocket. "I was a mistake."

Maggie pressed her lips together as if holding back something. He'd disappointed everyone this week. Amber, most of all.

"I'll be here tomorrow." He held her gaze and stepped closer. "You promised to let me make some mistakes. Well, this is one of them. I'm not perfect. I never claimed to be, no matter what this town tried to turn me into."

She didn't say anything, but she didn't withdraw, either.

The temptation was there. The longing to kiss her, to be with her. Was it totally physical or was there something more going on between them? Shaking those thoughts away, he brushed her cheek with his thumb. "I'll be here. I promise."

Chapter Fourteen

"Do you have the latest BlackBerry?" Brady looked over the small cellular phone offerings at the Electronics Hut in Owen. So much for getting his phone from Maggie last night. This morning it had slipped out of his jacket and a cow had crushed it to pieces with her hoof.

"We can order anything you need." The white-haired man behind the counter looked as if he had been at the invention of the phone.

"I was hoping to get something now." Brady glanced over the selection. He was hoping to download his information from the network, which would be easier with another Black-Berry.

"I got in a few new models…" The salesman seemed to drift off for a moment as if lost in a thought, or maybe he fell asleep.

Brady waited for a moment before saying, "Would you please check if you have a BlackBerry?"

"All right. Don't get your panties in a twist." The man

stood as if every joint fought against him. "I'll bring out what we have."

He moved slowly toward the stockroom, leaving Brady alone in the front of the store. He sighed and scanned the small store. Electronics of all sorts filled the shelves. What didn't fit on a shelf was shoved on the floor along the aisle.

The bell over the door jingled as the door slammed behind him.

"Where's Harry?"

Brady turned and saw a brown-haired man, about his age, struggling with a box of parts. He hurried forward as the box began to slip and caught the opposite end.

"Thanks."

Brady helped carry it to the counter. "What is all this?"

"Parts from a failed attempt at an electronics repair shop." They dropped it on the counter. The guy seemed familiar but Brady hadn't placed him. He held out his hand. "Josh Michaels. You're one of Luke's brothers. Brady, right?"

Brady shook Josh's hand, trying to place him. "In town for a few days. You graduated with Luke?"

"Yeah." Josh glanced around the shop, probably looking for Harry.

"The salesman is in the back. He should be out any minute." Brady hoped, at least. He needed to get back out to the farm and then Maggie's.

"White hair, looks like Rip Van Winkle?" Josh asked.

Brady nodded.

"That's Harry. You could be here for an hour before he finds anything in that storeroom." Josh settled against the counter. "How long has it been since you've been back?"

"Years." Brady picked up one of the phones and messed with the settings a little. "A lot has changed."

"The biggest blow was the Phantom Plant closing. Lot of good people had to move to find a job." Josh pointed toward his box. "The rest of us are just trying to make ends meet. Unfortunately, most people prefer to buy new than repair these days."

"I'm surprised they shut the plant." Brady hadn't followed the local news. With shrinking margins in most industries, downsizing seemed to be the only option.

"Businesses fell like dominoes in Owen after that. Money grew tighter until no one was spending anything and no one was hiring anyone." Josh nodded toward the back room. "Even old Harry threatened to close the shop. But I convinced him to carry cell phones. That seems to have brought in some traffic."

Brady turned over the cell phone in his hand. "Smart idea."

"One of my better." Josh smiled, obviously pleased with himself, but his smile fell. "Wish I could turn the whole town around. Get these people back on their feet and give them a reason to be proud again."

"It appears I have some time." Brady nodded his head toward the back room where they could hear Harry moving things around. As far as Brady knew, the old man might have forgotten he was out here. "Want to talk about some of your ideas?"

A few hours later, Brady's mind was churning as he headed toward Maggie's. Harry had called in a favor and should have a new phone for Brady by the morning. But what had him excited were the prospects for Tawnee Valley and the neighboring town, Owen. Josh had a lot of ideas. While some weren't great, some could work. If Josh could find a backer.

Brady had a lot of experience working on new projects and knew what it took to get them off the ground. He was already envisioning the layers of work that would be required to get Kyle to give the approval to go ahead with this project. Brady could help breathe life into this town and make his company a lot of money in the process.

There was almost an extra skip to his step as he walked to Maggie's front door. He felt invincible as if he could handle anything else that life intended to throw at him. What he wanted to do was sweep Maggie into his arms and forget to breathe for a while.

He pressed the doorbell and tried to squelch the half smile from his face. No one answered the door. He checked his watch. The bus should be arriving any minute. It wasn't like Maggie to be late, at least not in his experience.

He rang the doorbell again and waited. His elation from his good business sense was slowly fading to apprehension. What if something had happened to Maggie? What if something had happened to Amber? He didn't even have a spare key to get in to make sure everything was all right.

Leaning over the railing, he tried to peer into the window. Finally, he left the front and walked around back. Maggie's car was in the driveway. He could feel every muscle tensing in his arms and neck.

Whenever things seemed good in his life, something always happened. It was no one's fault, just bad timing. His mother's funeral had been two days before he was supposed to start college. His father had died the day before he turned sixteen. He got Maggie pregnant before he left for England and he didn't return until now to find out about Amber. Nothing good happened to him without a touch of tragedy.

He'd lost so much. He couldn't lose this, too. Not before he could figure out what it would mean to him. He pounded on the back door. They had to be okay.

"I'm up. I'm up."

He heard her over the pounding of his heart and tried to take a deep breath. The door swung open. Maggie stood in a pair of yellow pajama pants and a cat T-shirt with a robe hanging off her shoulders. Her hair was wild as if she'd been running her fingers through it and had attempted to pull it into a ponytail holder. Purple smudges highlighted under her eyes.

"Hey, Brady." No emotion entered her voice, but she looked like she hadn't slept in days or at least last night. Her eyes briefly glanced at him before her hand dropped off the door. She turned and shuffled toward the cabinets.

"Is everything okay?" Brady hesitated as he walked into the house and closed the door behind him. "Are you okay?"

"I'm just great." She emphasized the words with a huge yawn. She held a coffee cup. "Sleep is for wusses."

"Where's Amber?" He felt as if he'd walked into an alternate universe.

"She's in watching TV."

"Didn't she go to school?" Brady knew today wasn't a day off, which meant one of two things. His heart stopped inside his chest. "Is she sick?"

"It's a twenty-four-hour thing." Maggie waved her hand as if waving away his concern would be that easy. "We only have—" she squinted at her watch and sighed "—five more hours to go."

"Mommy!" Amber's voice was rough and had an edge of panic to it.

Maggie snapped to attention and changed before his eyes. The sleep was gone as she raced into the living room. He followed, trying to make sense of all of this in his mind. He'd left them last night and everything had been fine.

"It's okay, baby. Let's get you to the bathroom." As she passed him on the way, she seemed to realize he was there. "You should go home, Brady. You don't want to get sick."

Amber tried to smile at him but her face was pale and sweaty. They went into the bathroom and Maggie closed the door.

Brady stood undecided. Should he go? Maggie seemed to think so, but from the looks of it both she and Amber were on their last legs. He shrugged out of his jacket and draped it over the dining room chair.

Returning to the kitchen, he made short work of the few dishes in the sink and started some water to boil. The bathroom door opened and Maggie's murmured words caught his ear. He could almost imagine her rubbing Amber's back and saying those things only a mother could say when you were sick.

At seventeen, he'd done the same for his mother, trying to make her as comfortable as possible. But this was different. Amber was young and this wasn't cancer. Kids got sick all the time. His grip tightened on the plate in his hands.

She'd be all right.

"You're still here." Maggie sank into the chair at the table and laid her head on her arms.

"Yeah, I'm still here." He finished drying the plate and set it in the cabinet. "Where's Amber?"

"Sleeping on the couch." Maggie couldn't stifle the yawn that made the words come out nearly unintelligible. "You should really…"

Brady sat at the table next to her. "It's okay. I'm here. What do you need?"

Her eyes were shut but a partial smile lit her face. "Sleep."

He stood and lifted her out of her chair. Her eyelids popped wide-open for a second before lowering again. She put her arms around his neck as he carried her in his arms up the stairs.

She snuggled closer as he passed by the open door to Amber's room. Purple walls, a single bed with a purple-flowered cover on it, a shelf full of kids' books. Taped to the walls were art projects progressing from thick lines of paint in no particular pattern to recognizable representations of owls, monkeys, houses.

Hundreds of questions fell over each other to get his attention. Things he'd never thought of before. What was Amber's first word? When did she walk for the first time? Who had been there to catch her when she fell trying? What did she want to be when she grew up? How much time had Sam spent with her? Getting to know his niece? Who was going to hold her when someone broke her heart for the first time? Who was going to check out her dates to make sure they were good enough for her? Where would he be when her next firsts happened?

"You can put me down."

Brady gentled his hold on Maggie but didn't release her. Her hazel eyes were half-open. Who would be there for Maggie? "You're exhausted."

"Am not." Yawns bracketed her words.

One of the other doors had to be hers. He carried her to the next door and pushed it open. A light floral scent wafted over him. His fingers clenched into her. When he was sixty, he'd remember this scent, Maggie's scent. It tickled his nose and played with his senses, making him wish that Maggie weren't so tired and their child wasn't sick on the couch downstairs.

Draped in a multicolored quilt, a queen-size bed dominated the small, light blue room. The room was immaculate. Full of color. Almost picture-perfect. Just like Maggie.

Lowering her to the bed, he sat on the edge. Her eyes had drifted shut as she snuggled into the bed instead of against him. Coldness seeped into him where her warmth had been.

"Sleep, Maggie." He stroked a strand of hair out of her face. "Let me take on the responsibility for a while."

She mumbled in her sleep. He dropped a kiss on her temple before standing and heading downstairs.

Amber lay on the couch with a worn-out stuffed pig in her arms. She gazed at him with her wide, blue eyes. "Is Mommy okay?"

"Just tired." He moved to the end of the couch where her feet were and looked at her expectantly.

She pulled her feet in, leaving enough room for him. "At least I wasn't at school when I puked."

As he settled, she stretched out, her feet in his lap. "No one had to dodge your splattering?"

A small smile appeared. "You want to watch a movie with me?"

"Sure." For the moment, Brady was content to be with Amber and to let Maggie catch up on her sleep. Work pressed slightly at his mind, but he squashed it. Amber needed him to be here. Much as he hated to admit, the company would be fine without him even for a few hours or a few days.

Chapter Fifteen

Maggie stretched in bed. But when she opened her eyes, she could only make out the shadows of her bedposts and dresser. Bolting upright, she rushed out of her room and into Amber's. Her bed was empty. Her alarm clock read ten o'clock.

Downstairs. Amber must be downstairs. Maggie rushed down the stairs, not entirely sure she actually stepped on every tread. She barely noticed the dishes drying in the rack as she passed by the kitchen and stopped in the living room doorway.

The TV was barely loud enough to hear it, but that's not what caught her attention. Propped up by pillows, Brady was sprawled on her couch asleep. Amber was fast asleep tucked on the couch beside him with her head resting over his heart. A small wet spot had formed on Brady's black shirt under her slack mouth.

Maggie leaned against the doorjamb as her heart settled to a normal pace again. She glanced at the TV, which had returned to the main menu of the DVD that it was playing. *Rapunzel,* one of Amber's favorites.

No cell phone or laptop in sight. Had the New York Brady honestly watched a kid's movie without his precious phone to connect him to his office? Had he really carried Maggie upstairs and put her to bed? Warmth spread to her face. Had he seen her without makeup and her hair looking like a whacked-out version of Medusa?

Had she dreamed the gentle kiss to her temple? Lord knows, she'd had plenty of dreams about Brady, but none of those stopped at her temple.

A rustling brought her out of her head. She held her breath as Amber shifted slightly. Brady's snores died for a second. They both settled into sleep. Quietly, Maggie grabbed her camera and took a picture.

She slipped out of the room and headed into the kitchen to grab a bite to eat before she returned to bed.

"Brady says we can go to the park and maybe stop by Penny's to visit Flicker." Amber bounced in her seat at the table.

"Eat your pancakes." Maggie avoided looking at Brady as she put a plate of pancakes in front of him. He'd told them the story of his phone and the cow while she'd gotten the batter ready. Amber's appetite was back now that she was feeling better.

"How are you doing?" The words sounded almost tender. Holy crap, was that concern in Brady's eyes?

She stumbled slightly on her way to the stove. "I'm fine."

"If you need some more sleep, Amber and I can go to the park on our own. But we'd love it if you joined us."

She could hear the smile in his words even though she didn't dare look at him. How the man could sleep on a couch and wake up looking devilishly handsome was beyond her. She'd felt like night of the living dead last night. At least this morning, she'd had a chance to shower, put on some makeup and brush her hair before facing him.

His black hair was tousled. His clothes wrinkled and his shirt stained over his heart from Amber's drool. And all Maggie wanted to do was sit in his lap and feed him pancakes.

"I think they're done." Brady's voice shook her out of her fantasy.

She flushed as she plated the dark pancakes onto her plate. Thankfully, syrup fixed everything. She'd choke them down if she had to. She took her seat at the table across from Brady with Amber in between them.

"What do you think, Mommy?" Amber said around a bite of pancake.

Maggie was too distracted to chastise her about talking with her mouth full. "About what?"

"Coming with us, silly."

"Yeah, Maggie. Come with us."

Two sets of blue eyes were fixed on her. Amber's were wide and pleading; Brady's had crinkles in the corners as if he knew exactly what she had been thinking about and found it amusing. Give him a chance, he'd asked, and she'd agreed to it.

"Should I bring a picnic basket?" Maggie focused on Amber. It was a whole lot less confusing. Amber's eyes, while similar to Brady's, were still the eyes of her daughter. Looking at Brady stirred something within her and if he kept this new act up, she'd be in some deep doo-doo by the end of the day.

"I love picnics," Amber exclaimed.

"Me, too," Brady said, and without meaning to, Maggie looked at him. His face showed his pleasure. Yup, deep doo-doo.

Four hours later, Maggie found a shaded spot under an old oak tree to put out the blanket for their picnic while Brady pushed Amber on the swings. Amber had been swinging by herself for the past two years, but Brady didn't know that. Maggie shook her head as she set down the basket and drew out the blanket.

The air had a hint of nip to it, but it was pretty warm for a fall day. While there were plenty of leaves on the ground, the trees had held on to most of them. In a few weeks the trees would be bare. A good day to come to the park.

"Let me help you with that."

Maggie turned at Brady's voice. She glanced beyond him at Amber happily swinging away. "Did she have you fooled for even a moment?"

His carefree smile tugged at her heart. "Not a chance. Which is why I only pushed her a little, so she'd be done with me quickly."

He reached for an end of the blanket. She quickly passed it before he was able to touch her. She was having enough trouble breathing when he was around. If he touched her, she was fairly sure she'd forget how to breathe at all. And he being the Boy Scout he'd always been would be forced to give her mouth-to-mouth resuscitation. Her heart skipped a beat.

They backed away from each other to spread out the blanket. The whole morning he'd been thoughtful and attentive. A girl could get used to this if she weren't careful. Maggie tried to keep New York Brady in her mind, but even when he was angry at her over something, he turned her on and challenged her. The way he was acting today stirred the memories of the Brady she'd had a crush on since middle school.

Her heart still raced when he was near. The same way as it had back then. Even her skin prickled, waiting for an accidental brush or the touch of his hand. She wasn't a teenager anymore. This was ridiculous. The man turns on a little charm and suddenly she feels like putty? Just waiting for him to mold her.

She snapped the blanket to straighten it and lowered it to the ground. It wasn't as if she was innocent, or that he was all that great of a catch. She sat on the edge of the blanket.

"How's work dealing with you gone?" Maggie asked as she turned to dig out the picnic gear.

"Getting by." Brady's voice was near.

Looking over her shoulder, she saw that he'd stretched out on the blanket. All six-feet-something of him displayed like temptation itself. She needed to find something to remind herself that this Brady wasn't the real Brady. Fast-paced, self-centered, know-it-all was Brady now.

"I saw that you were talking to Jules when Amber got hurt…" *Take the bait. C'mon, you know you want to talk about work.*

"Yeah, one of the contractors was being a dick. Something about only wanting to deal with me." He didn't twitch a muscle.

"Aren't you worried she wasn't able to fix it?" Maggie set the plates next to the bowls of food she'd pulled out.

"Jules is a pretty competent woman. I'm sure she was able to handle herself." Brady finally rolled onto his side and looked at her. "Why are you suddenly worried about my work?"

She could feel the heat in her cheeks but kept getting things out and ready for lunch. "You've been without a phone for nearly two days and you haven't burst into flames yet."

He chuckled and the sound flowed through her. "Like I said, they are competent."

"And what brought you to that conclusion?" She lifted her gaze to his and wished she hadn't. His eyes were soft in the shade of the tree. A pretty deep shade of blue that should seem wrong on a man like Brady, instead sent a pulse of heat through her.

"I'd rather be here with Amber." He glanced toward the

swings. The chains creaked as Amber went back and forth. When he returned his gaze to hers, she inhaled. "And you."

Every unfulfilled wish came rushing back to her. How Brady would come sweeping into their lives at any moment and make things better. How her mother would have been cured and alive today. How Brady would love her.

But this wasn't wish time. She needed to remind herself of that and make him show her the truth. She dropped her attention to the food. "I bet you can't wait to go back to New York and your life."

"New York is good." There was hesitancy in his voice as though he was waiting for her to spring a trap.

"And your friends."

"Sure." Brady sat up and his attention on her made her wish for things that weren't real.

"And your girlfriends."

Only the sound of the creaking swing chains and rustle of leaves filled the void after her statement. Her breath caught in her throat, but she forced herself to continue with getting their lunch ready while waiting for his reply.

"Wow, that's one big land mine you placed right there."

"Excuse me?" She finally lifted her eyes.

There was a hint of anger in his eyes and God help her, if she didn't relax a little bit, even as her breathing hitched. Charming Brady might be difficult to manage, but she was used to angry Brady.

"I already told you that Jules and I aren't dating," Brady said carefully, probably negotiating the supposed *land mine* she'd put out.

"I know." She turned to watch Amber happily swinging. Hopefully, now he would tell her that there was someone in New York. That this was all fake and he was going to leave them.

"I don't have a girlfriend, nor would I want one in New

York. I have enough women in my life currently." He moved. She didn't see him move, but her body was in tune with what his did. His warmth drew closer to her. In the coolness of the shade, she longed to relax into him.

"I'm sure women are ready to toss themselves at you when you return." She managed to keep her spine straight and her tone even.

"What about you, Maggie?" His breath tickled the hair at the nape of her neck. Why had she put it up this morning?

"What about me?" Surely he didn't think she would fall at his feet. Because even if she believed he cared about Amber enough to stick around or even if he didn't care, at least felt a sense of obligation to Amber, Maggie wasn't about to fall into bed with him just because. She respected herself too much to sleep with someone without love. Didn't she? Okay, in New York, she'd gotten a little carried away, but lust was still lust. And it was intoxicating and tempting and arousing.

"Anyone in these parts float your boat?" His countrified accent caught her off guard.

"Float my boat?" Forgetting for the moment that he'd moved close, she turned to him. A breath separated them. A single inhalation would bring her flush against him. His eyes danced with a teasing, seductive light.

"Isn't that what the kids are calling it these days?" He gave her a half smile. Apparently, she hadn't been as off-putting as she'd tried to be.

It would be so easy to kiss him, but she wasn't about to let him win this match. "You must be the talk of the town with your pretty words."

"I get by." His head tipped oh so slightly to the left. An invitation if she'd ever seen one. His eyes said, "kiss me, I dare you." A challenge that she wouldn't accept if she had half a brain.

"I choose to keep it in my pants, as they say." She gave

him a tight smirk but didn't pull away like she should. It was like waving your hand over a flame. The closer you got to the wick the more danger there was of burning yourself, the higher the rush.

He glanced down. "That's a shame."

When he didn't look up right away, she followed his gaze. Her top gaped slightly from her turned position on the blanket, giving Brady a nice view of her cleavage and hints of the red bra she'd put on this morning.

He returned to look at Maggie. All the teasing was gone and his eyes were like the tropical ocean, warm and inviting. "Maggie, I—"

"Daddy, look how high I can swing."

For a breath he stayed where he was. She swore she saw something in his eyes that she'd never seen before. Something she wasn't sure she was ready to understand. The next breath he stood and walked over to Amber, shouting encouragement. She stared at him trying to decipher everything that had been said, and that look.

He had been nothing but sweet and charming this morning until she'd tried to pick a fight. He'd even turned that around on her. Every time they got close, it seemed as if the fire between them had only been smoldering and waiting for him to come closer so she could burst into flames. She had hoped that familiarity would dampen their lust. The day-to-day grind usually had that effect on relationships. Instead, the tension wound tighter and tighter. He didn't seem any less interested than he had in New York. In fact, he seemed more interested.

He glanced at her and caught her gaze. What had he been about to tell her? His lips curved into a smile. Her breathing hiccupped. Maggie swallowed. This day needed to end, because she was getting closer and closer to throwing herself at him.

"Time for lunch," she yelled.

Brady helped Amber slow the swing. Their laughter combined to make a perfect melody of sound. He wasn't here for Maggie. He was here for Amber. To get to know her, not Maggie. The tension eased out of her body. This was what she wanted for Amber. A father who loved her.

Chapter Sixteen

Maggie stood in the kitchen, staring out the window. Amber had insisted that Brady be the one to tuck her in tonight. Which probably meant conning him into reading her multiple books before bed.

Their picnic had gone off without a hitch. In the afternoon they'd spent a little time at Penny's with Flicker and then went grocery shopping, of all things. Maggie had been amazed by what Brady remembered from his days of working on the farm. He'd kept them both entertained with little stories about him and his brothers.

Amber had definitely fallen in love with her father, and Maggie couldn't blame her. Brady had proven today that he was still that boy she'd had a crush on in school. But he'd also shown her that the grown-up Brady was even better with more substance and a way of viewing the world that had to do with life and experience that neither of them had had eight years ago. Crushing on teenage Brady had been easy, but grown-up Brady made her feel unsettled.

"Deep thoughts?"

She spun around. Even knowing he couldn't read her mind, she felt vulnerable. As if she were latching onto an idea of what it would be like to do something insane like fall in love. With Brady.

"Did Amber go to sleep okay?" She had to find something to busy herself with. The dishes were done and put away. Everything was clean. Unless she wanted to pull out the oven cleaner and a scrubbing pad, there wasn't anything left.

"After five books." His smile was tender, as if he would read Amber a hundred books if she asked him to. "She was practically asleep when she asked for the fifth one. I made sure to read very slowly."

"Great." Oh crap, now what?

He looked as if he had absolutely nowhere to be. It was only eight-thirty. Maybe she should pretend to be tired and ask him to leave. She could watch some TV or work a little or…

"Do you want a drink?" Maggie blurted out. She had to say something, and everything else sounded rude after the day they'd spent together and especially last night with Amber. Besides, he just stood there watching her with a look that made her stomach flutter.

"Sure." His gaze never strayed from her as she went to the fridge.

She opened it and pushed things aside to see what she had. "I have some milk and juice boxes and water and a couple of cans of Diet Coke hidden near the back. Sorry, I don't normally have adult company besides Penny. So no real reason to drink."

But damn, could she use a drink about now.

"Water's fine." His baritone voice made her knees tremble.

She straightened and closed the fridge. With a forced smile, she walked over to the sink and flipped on the faucet to cool the water. "Water it is, then."

Her hands shook when she reached for the glasses. His hand curved around hers as his warmth engulfed her back. It would be so easy to go wherever this led them.

"Let me help you with that," Brady whispered next to her ear.

Shivers coursed along her spine, pooling into an empty pulsing between her legs. It was only lust. His other arm crossed her waist and pulled her tight against him. His hardness settled against her backside, leaving no doubt where his thoughts were.

Their hands closed over the glass, and he moved it to the stream of water. While the glass filled, his lips caressed the back of her neck. She forgot to think, to breathe as she succumbed to the desire that hummed to life whenever he was near.

He took the glass from her hand and set it on the counter before shutting off the faucet. Turning in his arms, Maggie met his gaze. His pupils were dilated. His breath shaky.

"No more games, Maggie." His fingers tipped up her chin as his mouth descended. There was no denying the chemistry between them.

His lips parted on hers, and she gave herself up to the feel of his mouth. The slide of his tongue against hers. The passion she'd been denying all week rose to the surface all at once. The kiss turned desperately passionate. She didn't want to think anymore, only touch him and let him touch her.

She pulled his T-shirt loose from his pants. Her greedy fingers found their way under to memorize the ripples of flesh beneath. As long as she kissed him, she wouldn't have to think, only feel.

Brady's hands had found their own way under her top, curving around her back before lifting her onto the counter. Not for one second did he release her mouth, and she didn't give him the chance.

It's as if they both knew if they paused for one moment, reality would come crashing in. His fingertips traced a path of fire beneath her shirt, making her skin tremble, anticipating his touch. She wanted to live in this moment. To ignore the warning bells going off in her head.

His lips trailed down her chin and his teeth grazed her throbbing pulse in her neck. The upper cabinets bumped against her head. No thinking. Thinking wasn't allowed.

But the kitchen? Not the best place in a house with kids.

"We…" she said.

His tongue found a spot on her neck that was as close to divinity as she had ever come. Even her toes curled in response to the flood of longing. Okay, just a second more and she'd stop.

The button of her jeans opened. Then she felt the tug of the zipper.

"Brady?" She tried again to be responsible, but his name came out as a soft moan.

His lips curved into a smile against her neck. He knew she was weak. Captured by his spell. Unable to untangle her thoughts long enough to think about Amber walking in on them.

That did it. She shoved against his chest and was surprised it actually moved him. His eyes were almost black and had that dazed look that she knew was reflected in hers. Their chests moved in time as they drew in much-needed air.

"We can't do this here," she finally managed to say.

"Maggie, you're killing me." His head dropped to her shoulder. His dark hair tickled her skin, keeping the fire on high.

"Brady, look at me." It was about time he actually heard her.

He raised his head and met her eyes before his gaze dropped

to her lips. She felt a corresponding tug deep inside. There
was no way she was turning him out tonight.

"Not *here*." She reached out and tipped his chin until he
met her eyes again. "Not in the kitchen. Amber might wake
up."

His eyes glowed like a child's at Christmas. "Well, why
didn't you say so?"

He swung her into his arms before she could make any
comment and strode across the kitchen and up the stairs. She
patted his arm until he lowered her softly to the floor in the
hallway. Grabbing his hand and hoping for the best, she led
him past Amber's door and into her room.

He towered over her and walked her backward until the
bed hit her knees. She grabbed his shirt as she lowered herself to the bed. He followed willingly. His lips met hers and
banished the other thoughts that had bubbled forth.

"Condom?" she mumbled against his lips.

He pulled out his wallet and withdrew a condom, placing
it on the nightstand along with his wallet.

"The door?" She had to cover all the bases while she was
still coherent enough.

"Shut and locked." He nibbled her bottom lip before kissing her senseless.

The sense of urgency took over again as she pulled his
shirt over his head. She could ignore the little warning bell
going off in the back of her mind. Especially when his mouth
was doing divine things to her neck. It didn't matter that they
hadn't discussed where they were going from here.

It hadn't mattered before, why should it matter now? Her
shirt followed his to the floor. His warm skin rubbed against
hers, and breathing became optional. She fell against the bed
as his lips worked magic along her collarbone. Her stomach
clenched as he worked his way closer and closer to her breasts,
which were confined by her bra.

Why shouldn't she be allowed this? So what if he'd be gone in a week? Shouldn't she enjoy what she could, like Penny always said?

His hands slipped beneath her and released the catch on her bra. With it out of the way, his mouth covered her nipple and she got her wish. Nothing but sensation flowed through her brain. He branded her with his mouth as his hands worked on her pants.

Want and need replaced everything. As his hands continued to explore her body, she nearly came off the bed when he switched breasts.

A small knock broke through the chaos of sensations. It was probably the house settling. Brady's finger teased her panty line.

Another knock followed by a small "Mommy?" had Maggie slamming her hand over Brady's and shoving him to the side. She took three deep breaths before grabbing a shirt and throwing it over her head.

"Just a minute." Suddenly, she was engulfed in Brady's rich scent. She had grabbed his shirt, still warm from his body. She held her finger to her lips when she looked at Brady.

He nodded.

Opening the door a crack, she saw Amber's face covered in tears. Forgetting everything, Maggie dropped to her knees and held out her arms. Amber flew into them, wrapping her arms tight around Maggie's neck.

"I...had a bad...dream," Amber said through her sniffles. Her arms stayed tight around Maggie and her head lay on Maggie's shoulder.

Maggie rubbed her back. Perhaps this was the universe saying *don't sleep with Brady Ward.* "It's okay. Why don't we go to your room and get you into bed?"

Amber's head shook violently on Maggie's shoulder. "I want to sleep with you, Mommy. In your bed."

Danger. Maggie tried to glance at Brady, but her head wouldn't turn far enough. Maybe he'd hidden in the closet. He could sneak out after Amber fell asleep.

"Can I call Daddy?"

No matter how many times Amber called him that, it shocked Maggie. She didn't know quite how to answer. After all, Brady was right there. No need for a phone call.

She wanted to laugh hysterically but instead her mouth opened and closed while she tried to think of some reason Amber couldn't call Brady besides the fact that he was in Maggie's bedroom.

"No need to call me. I'm here." Brady opened the door all the way and knelt beside Maggie. She cringed. What would Amber think?

Amber immediately released Maggie and flung herself at Brady. A stab of jealousy hit Maggie hard. She'd always been the one to comfort Amber. The one Amber clung to when she needed a good cry. The one Amber relied on to keep her safe.

And now Brady was hogging her glory. Not that she wanted Amber to have bad dreams. She just wanted to be the one her daughter wanted to comfort her.

"What happened to your shirt?" Amber asked. She snuggled up to Brady the same way she always snuggled with Maggie.

"Your mom was cold." Brady glanced Maggie's way. How could she begrudge him this when he looked so damned happy?

"That was nice of you." Amber pulled away and smooshed Brady's face between her hands, forcing him to look at her. "Would you stay and sleep with Mommy and me?"

"Of course." Brady didn't hesitate for a moment.

What the hell was going on in her life? First she about had sex with Brady and now she was about to climb in bed with him and their daughter? This was too weird.

Amber grabbed both their hands and led them to the bed. She climbed in and under the covers. "Mommy on this side and Daddy over here."

Not an ounce of the heat from before was in the look Brady gave her. It was questioning and tender. Almost as if he was giving her a choice. Oh, sure, Amber would blame her for driving Brady away.

Maggie shrugged and grabbed a pair of pajama bottoms from her dresser. After pulling them on, she climbed into bed with Amber.

"I don't even get my shirt back?" Brady smiled.

"I'm still cold." Maggie snuggled deeper under the covers. That, and it smelled like him. "If you aren't going to be comfortable, you could always go home."

"Wouldn't dream of it." He sat on the edge of the bed and took off his socks, but kept his jeans on. He lay on top of the covers, put his arms under his head and crossed his ankles.

"I'm glad you're my daddy," Amber whispered.

"Me, too," Brady whispered back.

Maggie reached over and shut off the lamp. As she lay wide-awake in the darkened room listening to the rustles and breathing of Amber and Brady, all the thoughts she'd put to the side while Brady had been kissing her rushed forward. But one question spoke louder than any of the others.

What if Brady wanted to be with Maggie because of Amber? All his charm and kisses were only to stay close to his daughter?

She felt a brush of his fingertips on her shoulder and tried to relax so he thought she'd fallen asleep. He wouldn't even be in her life now if it weren't for Amber.

Well, his charm and kisses wouldn't work on Maggie. She didn't need a man in her life and definitely not Brady Ward. She wanted a man who was in love with her for who she was. Besides, it wasn't as if she were already half in love with the guy.

His hand slipped away and immediately she missed his touch. Oh, for Pete's sake, she was better than this. Falling in love with the father of her child. Ha! Impossible because he lived in New York and she lived here. He was high class and champagne dreams. She was barbecue and beer.

Even if the chemistry was explosive, that kind of thing never lasted. Before long he'd resent her for holding him back. Especially since he didn't love her. Her heart throbbed and a warm well of tears choked the back of her throat.

He would never love her. Could she ever know if he really loved her? He would convince himself that it was the right thing to do. To love the mother of his child.

She drew in a shaky breath to keep from crying because she knew without a doubt that if she hadn't loved him before, she definitely loved Brady Ward now. And she couldn't do a damned thing about it.

Chapter Seventeen

Last night, this wasn't the way Brady had planned to wake up with Maggie. He stared across the bed and the tangle of dark hair at Maggie sleeping on the other side of Amber.

Her light honey hair spread over the pillow. The constant tension in her face had gone soft in sleep. He'd hoped they could ease some of the tension between them last night. The sexual tension had been building since New York and the only way to discharge it was to have sex. It was only natural.

It didn't help that she constantly battled him at every turn. Challenged him about his way of life. Stole his phone. Made him someone's daddy.

Instead of finally succumbing to the spark that hadn't died since they were younger, they'd ended up with Amber taking the middle of Maggie's queen-size bed. He'd never been kicked so much in his life, and he couldn't help but smile because of it.

The morning sun drifted in between the curtains and fell across Maggie's and Amber's faces. Amber had wanted her daddy to comfort her last night. Her heart had beat like a scared rabbit's against his. He'd forgotten to ask what her nightmare had been about. Wasn't even sure if he should ask.

Now she slept as beautifully as her mom. Even though Amber had his coloring, she had her mother's features. His heart was going to burst out of his chest. It almost felt as if they were a family.

What would it be like to have them with him? The thought startled him, but it had been in his mind all day yesterday. He had to return to New York and work. That's where his life was. But why couldn't he take them with him? Both of them.

Not just a week or two in the summer or a weekend a month, but forever. Maggie's nose crinkled in her sleep. Amber threw her arm across Maggie. Surely Maggie would see that they were better as a family. With Maggie there, he'd know someone was taking care of Amber while he worked.

It's not as if there was anything holding them to Tawnee Valley. Maybe the house, but Maggie's mom was gone. His brother lived there, but Sam wasn't exactly their favorite person.

Maggie stretched. Slowly her eyes opened and focused on him.

"Morning," he whispered.

She gave him a sleepy smile and stretched again. His shirt tightened against her body, giving him an image to dream about. If she noticed his interest, she didn't give it away as she rolled out of bed, careful not to disturb Amber.

Before he had a chance to say anything more, she was out the door.

"Do you like my mommy?"

Brady looked into Amber's wide-awake face. "Yeah, I like your mommy."

"Then why did you leave her?" Such a simple question but he didn't have a good answer to it.

His mouth opened as he thought of saying one thing, but then he closed it. He'd left because he needed to put his past behind him. He'd left to forget about a little town called Tawnee Valley where his parents had raised him and where they had died, leaving him and his brothers alone. He hadn't planned on leaving Maggie because she hadn't been part of the picture.

"I don't suppose you'd take an 'it's complicated, you'll understand when you're older'?" Brady tried.

From the look in Amber's eyes, she wasn't buying it. "Jessica says that when a man and woman don't like each other anymore, they move away from each other. But since you and Mommy like each other, why don't you live together?"

"Because Brady lives all the way in New York and our life is here."

Saved by Maggie's voice, Brady lifted his gaze as Maggie walked through the door in a different shirt. She tossed his T-shirt at him as she sat on the edge of the bed next to Amber.

Amber's face bunched up as she tried to work out her next question. Before she could ask anything more, Brady stood.

"I should go back to the farm." He tugged his shirt on over his head. Maggie's scent mingled with his.

"Sounds like a plan." Maggie didn't look as if she was going to offer to walk him to the door or anything.

"Can I come, too?" Amber bounced on the bed before turning her pleading eyes to Maggie. "Can I, Mommy? Please? I promise to behave. I can be ready. Please?"

"I don't mind," Brady said. "As long as you two don't have anything planned."

"No, we don't." Her smile seemed forced. "Go on, Amber. Get dressed so the two of you can go."

Amber hopped off the bed and rushed from the room. Doors opened and closed and drawers slammed before the sound of running water filled the silence between him and

Maggie. Picking at the blue shirt she wore, Maggie sat on the edge of the bed with her bare feet on the runner board. She didn't seem to be in any hurry to move or to talk.

"We should talk." Brady didn't know what else to say, but they really did need to talk about many things. He needed to sort through what he wanted on his own before he gave her his plan.

"About what?" She tried to give him a blank look, but he wasn't buying it. They hadn't discussed what type of arrangement they were going to have after this week or the fact that every time he was alone with her he wanted to touch her and kiss her.

"About a lot of things. Have dinner with me tonight?"

"We have dinner every night." Maggie pulled a length of her hair through her fingers. "When you aren't too busy working."

"Not here. Not with Amber. Out."

That finally got her attention. Her hands dropped to the bed as she looked at him. "Where?"

"Well…" Brady hadn't thought that far ahead. They needed neutral territory to talk things through, for him to have a chance to propose the arrangement and for them to discuss how to implement it. "How about we go to the restaurant in Owen on Main Street?"

No one ever called the place by its current name. Through the years it had been through so many owners and name changes that it had become that place in Owen on Main Street. It was practically the only sit-down restaurant for miles besides the small café in Tawnee Valley.

The only other restaurants were at least an hour's drive away. Brady could think of better things to do with their time than driving to get to a good dining place.

Maggie kept smoothing that one strand of hair. For a moment he thought she wasn't going to answer him at all. It wasn't that far-fetched that he would want to take her out to talk. Especially after last night.

"Okay." Maggie didn't lift her gaze from staring at the ends of her hair.

That was it? Too easy, but he could use a little easy right now. "Great, I'll pick you up at six."

"Who will watch Amber?" Suddenly, her attention was fixed on him. The sunlight glinted off the green in her eyes.

"Oh…" Who would watch Amber? He'd never thought about that. Never had to think about it before.

The water stopped. He only had a few minutes before Amber returned.

"What about Penny?" Brady didn't know Penny all that well. Only what Luke had told him once after a few beers in London. But she didn't seem like that bad of a person. Maggie trusted her. Amber liked her.

"Penny can't on Sunday nights." Maggie padded over to her dresser.

"I'll take care of it." Brady had to find someone. If all else failed, there was one person that owed him about eight years' worth of babysitting.

After a quick stop in Owen to pick up his new phone, Brady and Amber drove the country roads to get to the farm. Brady wished he could watch her face as she took in the countryside, but he kept his eyes on the road.

As he pulled in the driveway, Barnabus started barking and pretty soon the puppy joined Barnabus and started howling.

"Is that Flicker's brother or sister?" Amber leaned her forehead against the passenger-side window to see the balls of fur pacing the car as Brady took it easy over the gravel.

"Sister, I think." Brady parked the car near the old windmill.

"Is it okay to get out?" Amber's voice was timid, but trembled with excitement.

"They won't hurt you." Brady smiled reassuringly. "Just walk as if you have every right to be here and if they get in your way, give them a gentle push and say 'get down' firmly."

She nodded solemnly and opened the door. Immediately, two noses came through the opening and pushed into her lap. Her giggles filled the car as Brady leaned across her to shove the dogs back.

"You don't happen to have a pork chop in your pocket, do you?" Brady said. The dogs were wiggling and pushing regardless of Brady trying to shove them away.

"No." Amber laughed as the puppy licked her face.

A high-pitched whistle made both dogs retreat. Brady watched as they ran across the courtyard toward the barn and Sam.

"That was funny." Amber shoved out of the car and followed the dogs.

Brady hurried after her.

"Hi, Mr. Ward." Amber stooped to pet the puppy, who sat close to Barnabus and wiggled. Sam had trained the puppy quickly.

"Mr. Ward?" Brady gave Sam a questioning look as he caught up with Amber.

"He brings the baby animals to the petting zoo at the end of the school year," Amber explained, not paying any attention to the two men. Her focus was intent on the puppy. Barnabus whined and nudged her with his nose. She giggled and started to pet both dogs at the same time.

The color rose on Sam's neck. "Mrs. Potter asked me if I wouldn't mind. It's before planting season."

"Amber?" Brady tried to pry her attention away from the dogs. Finally, she looked at him expectantly. "Sam is my brother. He's your uncle Sam."

That finally got her attention. She stood and stared at Sam. "I've never had an uncle before."

"You have two. Your uncle Luke is away at college." Brady held his breath as Sam and Amber regarded each other. It was as if they were sizing up the competition. Each taking the other's measure. If she were a grown-up, it would have been intense. But since she had to tilt her neck so far to look at him, it ruined the effect.

"Sarah Beth says her uncle takes her to Dairy Queen on Sundays." Amber crossed her arms over her chest.

"We put little girls to work out here." Sam matched her pose and didn't seem as if he would budge an inch.

"If I work, do I get Dairy Queen?" She raised her eyebrow.

"If you do your job and don't complain, I can see what we can do." Sam couldn't possibly mean for Amber to do chores. The type of chores they used to do as boys were too much for a little girl.

"She's only—" Brady protested.

"I don't do windows," Amber said with all the calm of a seasoned negotiator. Brady had seen corporate negotiators with less talent.

"Neither do I. Do we have a deal?" Sam held out his hand.

She took it and shook it once. "A deal."

"Sam, you can't use my kid as child labor." Brady couldn't help but feel betrayed. He'd brought Amber out here to play not to be put to work.

"A promise is a promise, Daddy." Amber smiled at Brady before turning to Sam. "What do you want me to do?"

"This is insane." Brady threw up his hands.

"The baby lambs need to be fed. First, we need to go warm the milk and bottle it." Sam started toward the house and Amber followed. "Then we go out to the barn and feed them. Think you can handle that?"

"Yup."

Brady stood in the driveway with the two dogs. He couldn't help but wonder what had just happened. Since when did

Sam hang out with kids? And how did he manage to make Amber feel needed by giving her something she would have done, anyway?

"You let Amber go with Brady out to the farm?" Penny pushed the bowl of chips closer to Maggie. "You need these more than I do."

"I can't keep spending time with him. I almost had sex with him last night." Maggie slouched on the couch. The TV buzzed with a repeat of a show about house hunting in the background. Neither of them were watching it, but it seemed natural to have it on.

"Whoa, back up the bus, lady." Penny sat up on her knees from her curled position in the corner. "What do you mean *almost?*"

"Amber had a nightmare and then we all ended up sleeping in my bed. It was so freaking domestic, it was scary." There had been part of her that had been grateful that she hadn't been the only one carrying the burden of Amber's fears.

"Okay, we'll deal with that in a minute." Penny hit the off button on the remote. "Let's talk sex."

"It was nothing." Why she'd felt the need to confess, especially to Penny, she'd never know.

"That bad, huh?" Penny patted Maggie's knee sympathetically.

"No." Maggie couldn't seem to stop herself. Maybe Penny could sort out this mess. "It would be easy just to have sex. The tension is there. All. The. Time. I know now that he won't leave Amber because of my stupidity, but I think I want it to be more than it was before."

"You mean more than just sex?" Penny relaxed against the corner. Her forehead crinkled as she tapped a finger to her lips thoughtfully. If she'd come to a conclusion, she kept it to herself.

"Yes, more than sex. More than hey, you're my baby's daddy, why don't we knock boots." Maggie pulled the elastic from her hair and straightened her ponytail before slipping the elastic back on it.

"That's a good one. Knocking boots." Penny raised her eyebrow and quirked her lips into a smile.

"I'm afraid." Maggie put the bowl on the coffee table and stood. All this energy pulsed through her.

"You're always afraid."

"What?" Maggie hadn't expected Penny to say that.

"Think of everything you've been through." Penny ticked each thing off on her fingers like a grocery list. "Your father left, your mother's cancer, your unexpected pregnancy. We both know that it was awfully suspicious when Sam dropped off the money the first time. But the fact is, you were afraid of Brady then and you are afraid of Brady now. Because you love him."

Maggie's heart felt as if it was going to crumble into bits in her chest. "It doesn't matter."

"Why doesn't it matter, Maggie?" Penny finally stood. "Because the Brown women never get what they want? Because your mother couldn't make your deadbeat father stay? Because you're afraid to love anyone who isn't obligated to love you back?"

A touch of anger scorched the pity party happening in her body. "I love *you*. And you aren't obligated to love me."

"But I've always been there." Penny flipped her red hair. "And you have no reason to believe I'm going anywhere. But Brady is only obligated to Amber."

Tears welled in Maggie's eyes. "But what if he feels obligated to me because of her? What if everything he thinks he feels for me is only because of her? He doesn't love me. I would know it."

Penny grabbed a tissue box from the coffee table and held

it out to Maggie. "How would you know? You are so blind you couldn't even tell you've been holding out for Brady for the past eight years."

"That's not true—"

"Really?" Penny narrowed her eyes. "Not one date—a date, Maggie—has been good enough for you since you found out you were pregnant. You hid behind your mom's illness and then your daughter. It's time to stop hiding, Maggie."

Maggie breathed in deep. Everything Penny said touched at the heart of the matter.

"What happens if you put yourself out there?" Penny grabbed Maggie's hand. "What happens if you sleep with Brady and he doesn't want you anymore? It'd be freaking awkward for a while, but you'd get over it and so would he. But what if he wants you?"

That feeling of drowning came upon her quickly. She'd felt it before when she'd found out about her mother's cancer. Overwhelmed, confused, but she'd found clarity in one moment. One moment that had cost her. A night with Brady Ward. It had been impulsive and she'd paid for it. She would never regret her daughter. Amber was her life.

"I keep asking the same question, but you never give me the right answer." Penny sat on the couch and grabbed the bowl of chips before resuming her position in the corner.

"What's the answer, then?" Maggie wanted this to be over.

"The worst thing that could happen is that you could never try to be with the man you've loved since high school. That you let him go because you are too scared to find out that he might love you, too."

Chapter Eighteen

"You left her with Sam?" The accusatory tone in Maggie's voice couldn't distract Brady from a dressed-up Maggie. Her red dress wasn't particularly fancy, but it hugged her in just the right places, making his thoughts less than pure.

"Sam promised her Dairy Queen, a movie and chores in the morning. Besides, Sam owes me a lot more than one night." Brady offered her his arm. "Are you ready to go?"

She hesitated for a moment, almost as if she wanted to bolt up the stairs and hide in her bedroom. Instead, she gave herself a slight shake, which made her dress dance around her knees. "I'm ready."

He led her to his rental car and opened her door. All afternoon he'd worked on the logistics of how to get her to New York. He'd even put together a presentation. More for himself than her. It was the way he worked through things. It was comfortable.

He climbed in and started the car, turning the music to a soft volume. Now that he was with her, all the preparation flew out the window with one look at that dress. The soft floral scent that emanated from her didn't help the tightness in his pants. He'd be lucky if he could get through dinner— let alone the important conversation they needed to have— before he kissed her.

They had fifteen minutes to drive to the restaurant, an hour to eat, then the drive back before he could kiss her. When he kissed her tonight, unless she objected, he had no intentions of stopping.

"Did Amber enjoy the farm?" The thought of his daughter cooled him.

"She fed the lambs, and Sam let her try milking a cow." Brady pulled away from the curb as he told Maggie all about the "pet" cow that Amber spent the better part of an hour trying to milk. By the time they reached the restaurant, he was completely in control.

The hostess sat them in a booth toward the back. Very few people were in the restaurant.

"I think last time I was in here it was a barbecue joint," Maggie said from behind her menu.

"Looks like they decided fried chicken might work better."

"Until next week." Her smiling eyes peeked over the menu.

He couldn't resist returning the smile. The waitress came over and took their order. When she left, she removed the menu Maggie had been hiding behind.

Maggie smiled at him and it seemed as though she wasn't hiding anything like she normally did. Her makeup was subtle, but her hazel eyes seemed even more intense than normal, and a slight blush touched her cheeks. Almost the same flush she had after they kissed.

"You wanted to talk?" Maggie closed her hands on top of the table.

"We need to figure out where we are headed and what situation would be best for Amber." This was what Brady was good at, presenting a solid plan to corporate for a new venture. He never felt nervous about it anymore, but now his stomach twisted slightly.

"We're both adults, Brady. I think we can come up with some arrangement that makes sense." Maggie leaned forward. "I'm glad you want to spend time with her."

"I hope I'll always be part of her life."

"Of course. We could probably come out to see you for a few weeks in the summer. Maybe you could come here for holidays. Since Sam is here. We usually have holidays with Penny."

"I was hoping for more than that." Brady interrupted her flow, which seemed to throw her off balance for a moment.

"More?" Maggie sat against the booth back and grabbed the locket around her neck. "You mean like a month in the summer?"

"No, Maggie, I mean—"

"Here we go." The waitress put down the plates, oblivious to the fact that she'd interrupted them. "Can I get you anything else?"

"Not for me," Maggie said.

"Thank you." Brady waited until the waitress was gone.

Maggie picked at her food. Tears hovered in her eyes when she lifted her gaze. "I can't let you have her for half the year. It's not going to happen. She's my life. I know that's not fair to you, but I can't."

He reached across and grabbed her hand. "I'm not asking you to, Maggie. I would never take Amber away from you."

Her chest rose and fell as she searched his eyes. She drew in a deep breath and nodded. "I'm sorry. I assumed that's what you were building up to."

"You have every reason to want Amber with you. I can't imagine missing one more day of her life." Brady took a bite of his chicken, trying to figure out the easiest way to propose his suggestion. She wasn't a CEO. She was a woman who had an emotional attachment to what he wanted. If he had some way to convince her that if they went through with his plan everything would be fine, he would tell her. But it might fall flat. He didn't think it would, but there was a small chance it could.

She watched him warily as she nudged her mashed potatoes around her plate.

"Remember at Luke's party, I couldn't find a way to tell Sam that I wanted to take the internship in London?"

Confusion lit her face. "Haven't we been through this—"

"Bear with me." He smiled to reassure her. "You approached me when everyone else at the party ignored me."

"Nobody was ignoring you."

"Okay, avoided me." He winked at her to try to put her at ease, but his heart warmed from her rising to his defense. "I wasn't exactly good company that night, but you sat and listened. I'd barely acknowledged your presence in high school, but you listened to me. Instead of telling me my dreams were ridiculous, you encouraged me to follow them."

"Everyone knew you were going places, Brady. You didn't need me to tell you that." Maggie tucked a lock of hair behind her ear.

"But I did that night." Brady took in a deep breath. "I needed someone to tell me it was okay. That running away from my brothers didn't make me a bad person. Not that I asked you that, but you made me feel like I was making the right decision. Even if it was for the wrong reasons."

"What is wrong about wanting to go to college?" Maggie had stopped the pretense of eating and intently listened to him.

"It wasn't just the opportunity that I wanted." He swallowed. "Only Sam knew the truth of it."

Her brow furrowed, but she reached out a hand to him.

He accepted her offer and tangled his fingers in hers. She gave him strength. She deserved the truth. "I was running away, Maggie. I couldn't stay in Tawnee Valley after my parents were gone. Everywhere I went they were there, but they weren't anymore. The constant reminder was driving me nuts. I was weak. I couldn't have Sam and Luke relying on me."

"They did okay." Maggie squeezed his hand.

"Luke had a rough time of it and Sam was too controlling for his own good. But none of that matters now." Brady shook off the past. "I wanted you to know that I've run in the past, but that I don't plan to this time."

"What are you saying, Brady?"

"Come to New York with me. You and Amber. We'll find a good school for her."

She started to pull her hand away.

"We don't have to sleep together. I can find a bigger place, if you want. But I can't deny that I want to be with you. To see where this thing between us can go. Aren't you the least bit curious?" Brady could almost see the shutters shut over her eyes as she closed him out.

"Curious?" Maggie finally pulled her hand back. Touching him did funny things to her brain. Made her hear things that surely Brady hadn't said.

"Amber would be better off with two parents who loved her, right?" Brady's blue eyes turned calculating.

"I'm not denying that Amber needs both of us. But New York is far away..." Would it be so bad to go with him? To stop hiding like Penny thought she was doing?

"We'd be there together. I can help both of you through the transition." Brady reached across the table but she pulled her hands into her lap.

Something was wrong with what he was saying. If he touched her, she wouldn't be able to figure out what it was.

Everything he said was what she wanted to hear. Almost everything.

"What happens when we don't want to be together?" Maggie folded her arms across her chest. "What if all we have is a shared past, a child and lust? What if that isn't enough?"

What if she wanted love?

"It's a start, isn't it?" Brady straightened. "We don't have to decide anything tonight. You can take a few days to think it through. I want you and Amber with me, Maggie."

"We're supposed to leave Tawnee Valley and everything we've ever known to run off to New York and start over?" Maggie couldn't wrap her head around it. "Where would I work? What if things didn't work out? I couldn't support Amber and me in New York."

"Think it over. Please, Maggie. The one regret I have is not knowing what you were going through." Brady held up his hand to get the waitress's attention. "Let's go somewhere and talk. Not here, okay?"

She nodded. He hadn't offered her love. Not even marriage. Even though she had pushed it aside for years, she wanted the whole package. A man who loved her. A marriage that would last until they were old and gray.

He wasn't offering that. He was offering her a maybe. Maybe this could grow into something, but what if it didn't? What if he never loved her the way she loved him?

Before she knew it, they were in his car parked outside her house. Neither of them made a move to leave the car. His fingers curled around the steering wheel.

"Would you tell me what happened during those years?" Brady didn't look at her but stared ahead with his head resting against the car seat.

She undid her belt and shifted in the bucket seat until she was comfortable. "Do you want the long story or the short?"

"Whatever you are willing to tell me." Brady dropped

his hands into his lap and turned his head to her. "You're an amazing mother. Any fool could see that. But I know that wasn't your only struggle. I want to know you, Maggie. Not the brave facade you put on for the rest of the world, but you."

She breathed in deep. How much should she tell him? What did he really want to know? "I found out about my mother's cancer a month before graduation. I think I was still in shock by graduation. I canceled my college plans including the scholarship I'd worked hard to get. My friends were leaving, and all I could do was hope that treatment worked for my mom. While they were going off to begin their lives, I was staying behind to save hers."

"We don't always get a choice." Brady held out his hand and she took it. "Knowing someone might die is difficult."

"At the party, I wanted something I could have control over. I wanted to find out if the guy I had a crush on for as long as I could remember might possibly want me, too." She smiled softly in the dark, remembering the fanciful, romantic thoughts she'd felt that night.

"And then you found me?"

She squeezed his hand. "I went searching for you. All I could think was how this might be the last time I did something for me. Something entirely selfish. Something I'd wanted for so long."

His thumb stroked over the back of her hand. In the weak streetlights, she caught his gaze.

"You were leaving. I knew it was a one-time thing. I wasn't trying to trap or trick you."

"I know." Brady's low baritone sent shivers down her spine.

"I found out I was pregnant when I was as sick as my mother after her therapy. I didn't know what to do. I didn't want you to think I did it on purpose. I didn't want you to think I needed you. So I wrote a damned letter." She laughed self-deprecatingly. "A letter I hoped you never received. But when Sam brought me money, I didn't question anything."

His fingers tightened on hers, but he stayed quiet.

"We needed the money. I wanted to believe you were that type of guy. The guy who thought throwing money at a problem made it go away. Because it would be easier to lose you if I never had you. I knew what Mom had gone through with my dad and I was scared." She used her other hand to wipe away a tear that slipped out.

"Amber was born. Mom went into remission. Things were good for a while. When Mom got sick again, we had a rough year and then it was over. She was gone."

"And you were alone again." He reached out and brushed another tear from her cheek. His hand cupped her cheek, making her feel cherished.

"Amber and I carried on. The end." If only it had been that easy. If only it hadn't been a constant struggle for her.

"You're a wonderful person, Maggie." His soft words startled her.

She searched his eyes for the hidden meaning behind his words. "I kept you from your daughter for eight years and you think I'm wonderful?"

"You were protecting yourself and Amber." Brady touched his forehead to hers. "We all run away sometimes. In our own ways."

He was right. She hadn't run away physically but she had emotionally. Too afraid that the voices telling her he would hate her would be true. Too afraid that he didn't want Amber.

Now he wanted them both to go to New York with him. She'd never considered that he'd want them as a package deal. She'd never considered that he would want them at all.

Could he learn to love her? She pressed her lips to his. The brief touch sent warmth throughout her body. She loved him. Maybe not when she'd been eighteen, but the man he was now, the one she'd gotten to know over the past week. In all her life, she'd never loved anyone the way she loved Brady. He made her think. He made her laugh. He made her sigh with pleasure. He made her feel as if everything would be okay as long as he was in her life.

"Let's go inside," she whispered. The decision for New York could wait until morning. Denying that she wanted him was only driving them in circles.

"Are you sure?" His thumb caressed her cheek. His blue eyes searched hers.

"Aren't you?" She leaned into his hand. They both needed to heal and they needed the other to help. Even if it was only one more night, she wanted this.

Chapter Nineteen

Maggie held Brady's hand as they made their way upstairs to her bedroom. No disruptions tonight. No mindless passion.

Tonight Maggie would give Brady her heart the only way she knew how.

He turned her until they were face-to-face. "I've always wanted you, Maggie."

Want. Lust. Desire was easy. Just standing next to him had her pulse racing, her nerve endings waiting for his touch, her breathing choppy. His thumb traced a path of fire over her bottom lip.

She met his eyes and began unbuttoning his shirt. No rushing. No hurry. Every moment would be savored and remembered. His blue eyes glittered in the dim light of her room. His hands smoothed over her shoulders. He paused at her zipper and lowered it until his hands reached the base of her spine.

Helping him shrug out of his shirt, she never broke eye contact. It kept her centered, reminded her that this was for her heart. To be with Brady and see if she could stand loving him, when he didn't love her in return.

He drew her closer and lowered his lips to her forehead. Light kisses trailed over her face, closing her eyes and making her body pulse with need. When his lips finally took hers, she drew in his breath as her own.

The urgency of last night was forgotten as he sipped slowly on her lower lip. As he rediscovered her mouth, his fingers slipped through her dress's open back and touched the trembling flesh beneath.

She didn't want to hurry, but her body was beyond ready to move to the next step. Her fingers threaded through his hair as she deepened the kiss. He followed her lead and slipped the dress from her shoulders. She kicked off her heels without relinquishing his mouth.

This time wasn't about hiding behind passion. Or even about succumbing to a chemistry neither of them could deny. This time she wanted the way her lover touched her, the way he kissed her as if it were the last time they would be together or the first, to touch her soul.

The rest of their clothes followed the dress and shoes. Each piece brought a new sensation until nothing but air separated their bodies. Her breasts pressed against his lightly haired chest. Her stomach shivered inside as it pressed against his heat.

And yet his hands remained low on her hips. He wanted her to lead this dance. She broke off the kiss and gasped in air, causing her body to fit tighter to his.

He groaned as he kissed the side of her neck. "You are so beautiful," he muttered against her skin. His fingers flexed into her hips, pulling her tight against him.

Fire and heat coursed through her veins, pooling between her legs. She pulled away from him slightly and caressed the stubble growing on his cheek. The words *I love you* hovered on her lips, longing to be released. To share with him the joy and fear, but she couldn't.

"I've waited a long time for this." She pulled the covers back on the bed and held her arms out to him. "Do you remember what you said to me that night?"

Closing the distance between them, he wrapped his arms around her. Her ear rested against his beating heart. She wondered if hers pounded like his.

"I said that I wished I hadn't wasted my time." He kissed the top of her head. "That I'd really seen you when we were in school."

He tipped her chin up and lowered his lips until his barely touched hers. "That we had more time."

"We have time now." Maggie met his gaze, hoping he could see how much she wanted him to love her. Knowing it left her vulnerable but not caring.

"We have the rest of our lives." His words sent a shock wave through her being as his lips claimed hers. They moved together on the bed, connected lips to lips until they lay beside each other.

She forgot to breathe as his hand wandered over her breast, encircling her nipple until it hardened. When his hand left her, his mouth claimed her other breast. His fingers drew circles down her belly until he cupped her in the palm of his hand.

The need to touch him, to give him the pleasure he was giving her, filled her. Her fingers traced over his tightened abs and caressed his hip bone. His moan made her smile, but then he changed positions, taking her other breast into his mouth. Her breath hitched. His fingers moved over her until she could think of nothing but the next touch, the next sensation. The heat built until she feared she'd burst into flames if something didn't change soon. If he didn't let her find the release that had been building for the past week.

Her fingers closed over him and he stilled. His harsh breath bathed her breast in warmth. She explored him with the lightest touch. His tongue flicked out at her nipple. His hand resumed the slow tortuous pace until her hips rose to meet him.

It was right there, so close she could almost touch it. He moved up her body and took her mouth with his. She clung to him as her body burst with sensation and pleasure.

Her breath caught as he caressed her breast. The fire started to rise within her again. He shifted on the bed until they were chest to chest, stomach to stomach, thigh to thigh.

He made short work of a condom. When he lifted his head, his eyes were liquid pools in the darkness. She could feel her heart quietly singing as his thumb stroked her cheek.

He entered her slowly, making their bodies one. Never once taking his gaze from hers. She needed to see his eyes, to see if there was even a little hope that he could love her. A little hope that she could cling to as her heart broke.

As he moved within her, the flames built until thought became impossible. His lips found hers in the storm and they clung to each other, reaching for something just out of their reach. In this moment, they made sense. They fit each other perfectly. Matched each other unlike anything else she'd ever felt. As they climbed closer, he held her tighter, and her heart wished it was because he was afraid to let her go.

Sparks burst behind Maggie's eyes as a new rush of sensation flowed through her and she felt him join her as they were engulfed.

Brady woke slowly, a little disorientated in Maggie's bedroom. Maggie's warmth covered his side, and her hair tickled his nose. They must have fallen asleep at the foot of the bed. Covers were thrown over them and spilled onto the floor.

He hugged Maggie to him. For once, his heart felt settled. This felt right, having Maggie with him. Last night had been amazing. There hadn't been the normal awkwardness of sleeping with someone for the first time. Granted it wasn't their first time, but it had been eight years.

In a week, he could have Maggie and Amber in his apartment in New York. He'd written an email to his assistant yesterday to start a folder on Josh's ideas for Tawnee Valley, including the files he'd started the other day. He'd also requested that the refrigerator in his apartment be stocked. He'd sent her a couple of pictures for the guest bedroom to be transformed into a little girl's room for Amber. Fresh flowers were to be in every room when they arrived.

Two weeks ago when he'd been preparing for the Detrex presentation with Jules for corporate, he would have laughed if someone told him he'd have a family in a week. It surprised him that he hadn't even thought about the project in the past few days. So consumed with Maggie and Amber that it hadn't been as important as it always had been. They could be a family. Brady hadn't had any part of a family since he was eighteen. He'd been driven to fill that emptiness with his career. Now he had Amber and Maggie.

He wanted to shout from the rooftops, proclaim to the world his happiness. Instead, he stared at the woman in his arms. Who knew Sam would be right years ago? Maggie was a keeper. Brady had been stupid to let her out of his life before. He wouldn't make the same mistake twice.

Maggie stretched and looked at him with sleepy eyes. "Morning."

Yup, this was how he wanted to wake up every day. "Morning."

She glanced around, noticing their feet near the pillows. She shrugged and put her head on his chest.

"Want to go over to The Rooster to get breakfast before going to pick up Amber?" He tucked his hands beneath his head.

She propped her chin on her hands to look at him. "You're lucky today wasn't a school day."

"I'm one of the luckiest men alive. Come on, we can't spend all day in bed."

If she had protested even a little, he would have stayed in bed with her all day. Instead, she sighed before getting up. The sunlight lit her skin in a golden haze. He sucked in a low whistle before she put on her robe and slipped out of the room.

A half hour later they sat in the only café in Tawnee Valley, where they served cholesterol with an extra helping of cholesterol and a side of burned caffeine. A few older farmers sat at the counter nursing their coffees. Brady was getting better at recognizing people. Bob Spanner had sold Dad a few head of cattle. Russ Andrews helped Sam with the crops in the west field. Guy Wilson's property abutted the Ward farm on the north side. Brady had run into probably half the town in his week here. Nothing changed in Tawnee Valley. It was comforting and exasperating.

He needed to put a spare set of clothes at Maggie's. Maybe he should bring his whole bag and spend the rest of this little vacation from reality with her.

He gave Maggie a smile that made her blush. Nothing could touch him this morning. Not even the email from Jules saying the project was going poorly in New York. He hadn't even felt compelled to answer right away. It could wait until this afternoon.

"Morning, Maggie and Brady." Their waitress was Rachel Thompson, who used to babysit Brady and Luke. "What can I get for you?"

"Two specials." Maggie handed the menu back. "Over easy with bacon."

"All righty. I'll have those up for you in two shakes." Rachel winked at Brady before sauntering off toward the kitchen.

"About New York…" Maggie didn't meet his eyes.

"Like I said, up to you if we sleep in the same room or not. You don't like the apartment? We can get a different one.

There's a few schools we'll need to contact to see if we can get Amber in on such short notice. I can have my assistant put together everything we need."

"Hey, Maggie." Brady recognized Josh's voice behind him. "We don't see you here often."

Brady stood and held out his hand to Josh. "Josh. Been meaning to call you."

Josh took Brady's hand, but stopped shaking it. His gaze darted to Maggie, then back to Brady. His light mood darkened. "*You're* the deadbeat?"

"Josh. This isn't the time." Maggie's tone was level and meant to cool things down.

"*Deadbeat?*" Brady repeated. He released Josh's hand. For some reason the connections weren't coming together for him. He and Josh had had a great conversation the other day. He'd even seemed pleased to see him for a minute. What was different now?

Maggie's eyes were huge, but she had that under-control look she had when taking care of a problem. Was there something going on between her and Josh?

"I always figured it was Luke." Josh glared over Brady's shoulder, obviously speaking to Maggie and not Brady.

Brady didn't like his tone. The other diners had stopped talking to see what was happening. What was Josh accusing Luke of?

"Not here, Josh," Maggie said through her teeth.

"Why the hell not, Maggie?" Redness seeped into Josh's face. "Oh, I even thought it was Sam for a while. But Brady?"

"It's none of your business, Josh." Maggie stood and moved to Brady's side.

"I'm missing something here," Brady said. Maggie's angry eyes locked with Josh's. He was keenly aware of the other diners and unlike in New York when they had been curious strangers, these people knew him, knew his parents, knew his brothers. "What do my brothers have to do with Maggie?"

Ignoring Brady, Maggie and Josh continued to have their silent battle, but it didn't seem to be getting them anywhere. The only thing he and his brothers had in common was looks. Like a spark igniting tinder, Brady's brain made the connection. This had to be about Amber.

"Why don't we calm down, have a seat and discuss this like rational people?" Brady gestured toward their booth. This wasn't an issue for the other diners.

"Seriously, Maggie?" Josh finally gave Maggie a disappointed look before turning his anger on Brady. "Do you know what kind of hell you put her through?"

"Josh, no." Maggie stepped forward, but Josh held out his hand.

"Do you?" Josh asked again.

"I have some idea." Brady straightened, ready for whatever came next. He'd already made amends with Maggie over the past. "I didn't know about Amber."

"Didn't know?" Josh turned to the people at the counter. "He didn't know, and that makes it okay."

"Josh Michaels, you cool it right now." Rachel came from inside the kitchen to stand next to Maggie.

"How can you all just sit there and watch? Eight years this woman went through hell. We were all here. We all saw. Grace Brown had been a loving, thoughtful woman. She'd loved that little girl with all her heart." He spun to Brady and shoved Brady's shoulders, but Brady absorbed the impact.

"All it would have taken was one phone call. One visit. And you would have known, but you were too busy in London to think about the girl you impregnated. And how devastated she was when her mother died."

"Maggie says it's none of your business." Had Brady been

so self-centered? So focused on forgetting that he hadn't had the decency to at least check on the people he'd left behind?

"I would have married her, if she would have had me," Josh spat out. "Because that's the right thing to do."

Maggie gasped.

What could Brady say? He hadn't been aware? All he could do was stand here and take it. Josh wasn't going to be done until he'd had his say. The tips of Brady's ears burned as every eye in the diner turned on him. What did they expect of him? What they always expected from him?

To be the better man. To be their champion. But in this case, he wasn't.

"I wouldn't have sent her 'hush' money." Josh looked down his nose at Brady.

The diner went silent as if everyone held their breath to see what Brady would say.

"Brady?" Maggie touched his arm. "Let's go."

"That's right, Maggie." Josh stepped away with his arms wide, inviting Brady to hit him. "Protect the man who did you wrong."

"Please, Brady," Maggie said.

Brady had never been the type to fight. He'd always solved his battles through negotiation. Luke had been the passionate one who had been in more fights than Sam and Brady combined. But in this case, Brady had no standing. He deserved whatever this man flung at him.

Brady took his gaze from Josh and searched Maggie's eyes. What had he done? What had he forced her to live through alone?

"Let's just go." Maggie tugged on his arm. "I'm sorry, Rachel."

"Men." Rachel seemed to think that was the most reasonable explanation.

Brady let Maggie lead him out. The stares of the people

who had once deemed him the golden boy of Tawnee Valley burned through him. He wasn't even worth their regard now. He'd used Maggie for one night of passion a long time ago and had never once thought about the possible consequences. He'd barely thought of her at all throughout the years.

When they were seated in the car, he said, "I'm sorry, Maggie."

It would never make things right. It wouldn't change the past eight years. But he had to try. He had to fix this.

"It's not all your fault." Maggie didn't meet his gaze.

"I never even checked to make sure you were okay. For all I knew you could have been killed driving home from our house at four in the morning." Those looks. Brady would never get them out of his head. Disappointment, disapproval.

"I could have tried harder to reach you. I knew you and Sam didn't get along." Maggie's voice was soft. When he turned to her, she was gazing out the window away from the diner.

She could have married Josh. Amber would have had a dad and maybe even some brothers and sisters. But she hadn't. She'd chosen to stand on her own.

"I admire you." The words came out softly, almost unintentionally.

Finally, her hazel eyes met his. Her smile was wistful as she took his hand. "Let's go get Amber, okay?"

It didn't matter what the town thought of him and Maggie. It mattered that she was with him now.

Chapter Twenty

The drive to the farm didn't dispel Brady's sour thoughts. With every mile, one fact burned in his mind. If Sam hadn't been such a control freak, Brady would have known about Amber from the beginning. Whether he would have returned or not would have been on Brady. He could have been the *deadbeat,* but they would never know.

When he parked near the house, the anger Brady had been repressing for years churned within his gut. Maggie had been silent the whole car ride.

"Why don't you go in and get Amber. I need to talk to Sam." Brady didn't wait for Maggie's reply before heading to the barn where music played.

He pushed open the barn door and stopped. Amber was in the process of painting a wooden chair while Sam tinkered with his tractor.

"Morning, Daddy." She smiled at him from her task.

"Morning. Why don't you run in and get cleaned up?" Brady waited while she rushed to the house.

Sam wiped his hands on a greasy rag. "That kid can sure pack away the food. I think she ate more than me."

The whole world was off-kilter this morning. First the diner and now Sam acting as if Amber had always been a part of their family. "Don't act like you like having my kid around."

"Why not? She's a good kid." Sam looked over the tools on the workbench.

"If you thought she was such a good kid, why wait eight years to tell me about her? All you had to do was tell Luke, if you were worried about being the first to cave."

"Is that what you think happened?" Sam was a little too cool for Brady's taste.

"Just another way for you to control everything on this farm." Brady paced the barn door opening. "You interfered with my life. With Maggie's and Amber's lives. Why don't you tell me what happened?"

Sam set down the tools as if he didn't trust having them in his hand before he faced Brady. "I was protecting you."

"By keeping Amber a secret? How the hell was that protecting me?" Brady could feel the burn on the back of his neck as anger pulsed through him.

"What would you have done if you'd known?"

"I sure as hell wouldn't have expected Maggie to take care of everything. I would have done something." Brady felt flustered. He had no idea what he would have done.

"For God's sake, Brady, Mom raised you better than that."

"Where do you get off—"

"Do you think my life has been all that great? Do you think I wouldn't have given anything to be able to get away for at least a while?"

Brady hadn't given it much thought. It had always been Sam who would take over the farm.

"I did everything in my power to make sure you and Luke were able to live the lives you wanted. Did I make some crappy decisions along the way? Hell, yeah. What do you want? I was only twenty years old with the responsibility of two younger brothers and a farm to deal with. I was happy Luke graduated at all."

"You didn't have to—"

"Didn't I? Think, Brady. Who did Mom turn to when Dad died? She asked me to stay and I did. I don't regret the decision, but sometimes I hate it. I hate the farm and I hate our parents for leaving me with everything."

"I tried to help."

"Your ambition has always outstripped this town. Did I want to see you get stuck here in a marriage you felt obligated to offer? Watch you turn bitter and disillusioned about life?"

"It was my life. My choice. You could have trusted me to make the right one." Brady's chest hurt as if Sam had punched him. "And even if I had been impulsive at twenty, why wait eight years before letting anyone know?"

Sam's lips tightened and his brow furrowed. He turned to the tractor without another sound.

His silence was the only proof Brady needed. As much as Sam had claimed he needed Brady, he hadn't wanted him around.

"Dammit, Sam. Not this time. You don't get to turn your back on me and act like a freaking martyr. If you aren't going to say anything, you might as well listen."

Brady took a deep breath to clear his mind. "Eight years. You could have told me anytime in eight years. You could have waited until I was older and time had healed whatever wounds I had, but you didn't. You owe an explanation to me."

"A month ago, I had to get a chest X-ray for insurance. My heart is enlarged, but since I don't have any other symptoms, I'm monitoring my blood pressure and going to the cardiologist in a month."

It felt as if the floor fell out beneath Brady's feet. "You're sick? Have you told Luke?"

"What? So he can stare at me like you are?" Sam moved around to the other side of the tractor, obscuring his face from Brady's view. "I'm fine. I feel fine. I thought you should know about your daughter since you came back to the States. In case something happened to me." Sam the martyr. Brady hated this side of Sam.

"We can't fix the past, Sam. What's done is done. I'm sorry I wasn't around to help more. I'm sorry that I left you to raise Luke on your own. I'm sorry you had to take on everything. I'm sorry about your heart."

"That's an awful lot of sorry," Sam grumbled.

Brady sighed. Sam wouldn't even lift his gaze.

"I know you won't say you're sorry for what you've done." Brady let the anger slip away. "But I forgive you."

"I painted a whole chair by myself," Amber proclaimed in the car.

Brady had been stiff and silent since the conversation with Josh at the diner. Maggie wondered if she should talk about New York. Last night had been wonderful, but it wouldn't work long-term. If she kept sleeping with him, she would fall deeper in love with him.

"Sam wouldn't let the dogs sleep with me last night, even after I threatened to sleep outside." Amber gave her prettiest fake pout.

"Dog kisses, yuck." Maggie made a face for Amber.

"When I'm older, I want to have ten dogs."

The car slowed to a stop at her house. Maggie dared a glance at Brady's profile. He seemed to be processing something.

"Here's my key. Amber, go inside and get ready for lunch."

Amber wrapped her arms around Brady's shoulders from behind. "Are you staying for lunch, Daddy?"

"Maybe, but I might have to go." He touched her arm with his hand. "We'll do something fun this week together. I promise."

"'Kay." Amber bounced out of the car. Within seconds, she disappeared into the house.

"You know what I can't get out of my mind?" Brady stared straight forward through the windshield and into the distance.

"No, I don't." But she wanted to know.

"How much better my life would have been if you and Amber had been in it all along."

Not exactly what she thought he would say. She couldn't keep it inside anymore. "We can't move to New York."

That got his attention. She wanted to clap her hands over her mouth and take it back.

"It's scary, Maggie, but we can make this work."

She took a deep breath. "I'm sure your life is great in New York. You don't know how flattered I am that you want me and Amber to be part of that, but…" She wished she hadn't put that disappointment in his eyes.

"We can take it slow. It doesn't have to happen right away." He traced the line of her cheekbone with the back of his fingers. "Think about it?"

"It's not going to happen, Brady," Maggie said firmly. "Our lives are here. New York isn't the best thing for Amber and me. I know how attached you've become to Amber. We'll visit and our door is open anytime you want to come down."

"Marry me."

"What?" She leaned against the car door.

"We have a wonderful daughter. We're obviously compatible in bed. It would guarantee that I wouldn't just leave you in New York alone. If that's what it takes to have you with me, that's what I'm willing to do."

Her heart stopped pounding for a moment. Had he just rationalized a marriage proposal? When she'd found out she was pregnant, she'd hoped for this. For him to offer to take care of her forever, but when he didn't show up, she'd had to become stronger and start taking care of everything herself. No one was going to sweep in and do everything for her.

"If you'd known about Amber, you would have proposed to me because it was the so-called right thing to do. But you didn't love me then, any more than you love me now. I would have said yes because I was scared out of my mind to be alone."

"It doesn't have to be about love. It makes sense for us to be together for Amber."

"Don't you see, Brady? I'm not scared anymore." She rolled her shoulders back and opened the door. "I've raised Amber on my own. I don't want 'good enough.'"

He opened his mouth.

Maggie smiled even as her eyes filled with tears. "I love you, Brady Ward. But I don't think you could ever love me the way I deserve to be loved."

Before he could change her mind, she slipped from the car and hurried into the house.

"Peterson has a meeting with Kyle on Wednesday. He wants to put an ax in our project."

Brady looked up at the sky, wondering why he'd suddenly become some butt of a cosmic joke. Everything seemed to be going wrong. The report on his computer screen claimed the project was aiming to go over budget in thirty days. That couldn't be correct. Brady had been diligent in making sure the budget was spot-on.

"Have you talked with Kyle?" Brady rubbed his hand over his hair and looked out over the farm from the top of the hill.

"I'm going to go in tomorrow morning, but your files have

disappeared from the server." Jules sounded as upset as he felt. "This project is going to die before it got started."

Which wouldn't look good for either of them since a significant amount of money had been spent up front. Brady had lost his brother and possibly Maggie and Amber. He couldn't lose his job, as well. What more could he do here? At least if he went to New York, he could fix the project. After all, it seemed as if work was the only thing he was good at.

"Schedule with Kyle for tomorrow morning. I'll call my assistant and book on the next plane out."

"Brady, you don't have to do that. Email me the files. I'll try to reconstruct what you did. You have your family to worry about."

Sam walked from the house to the barn. A small figure on the gravel drive below. Sam had almost sacrificed the farm to keep giving money to Maggie for Amber from what Brady sent home. Sam had given up his dreams so Brady and Luke could have a chance at theirs. He'd gone about it the wrong way, but he'd been as young and impulsive as they had been.

For once, Brady wanted to make Sam proud, to honor that sacrifice. This was what Brady was good at.

"I'll see you tomorrow morning, Jules." Brady hung up the phone. He double-checked to make sure the files weren't on the company server before logging out. A quick phone call and he was on the next flight headed to New York. He would save this project and he'd go on with life as it always had been. Maybe Maggie would come to her senses after a while.

But first, he had to say goodbye.

After several moments of searching through the winding rooms of the barn, he found Sam in the back garage. A stripped-down version of a '69 GTO sat on wheel ramps.

"Is this your old car from high school?" Brady strode forward to touch the silver hood. "I remember when you and Dad worked on it that summer."

"I remember you kept trying to help and how I wished you would just go away," Sam said from under the car.

"I felt the same way." Brady smiled at the memory. Each of them vied for their dad's attention but Sam had always won.

"I tried to go away."

"I'd almost forgotten about when you went to college." Brady leaned against the workbench in a space that looked a little less dirty. "You went to Iowa State. Mom and Dad were so proud. You'd only been there a week when Dad had his heart attack."

Sam rolled out from under the car and sat on the creeper. "I got home in time to say goodbye. Dad told me that you were all my responsibility now."

"You never told me that." Brady lifted a hammer that had been around the farm longer than he had.

"You didn't need to know." Sam rested his arms on his knees.

Brady let his gaze roam over the old car that he used to want so badly. He'd begged Sam to let him ride in it. Eventually, Sam had caved and took him around the back roads. It had been like flying. "I have to go back to New York. A situation has come up at work."

"You don't owe me any explanation." Sam's voice was gruff.

"Actually, I owe you an apology. I ran out on you and Luke, and when you didn't try to reach out, I thought you were telling me to stay away. I didn't mean for things to end up like this. I should have been here with you."

Sam stood. "I wished I could trade places with you. That you would be the one stuck on the farm with no escape, while I was the one living the good life somewhere far away.

"There's no need to apologize, Brady. I wanted you here, but I wanted you to have a better life outside of Tawnee Valley. To make something out of yourself and make our parents proud."

"They'd be proud of you, Sam." Brady took in a deep breath inhaling the smell of old oil and grease and that slight hint of dirt. Things that would always make him think of his dad and Sam. "Why didn't you tell me about all this?"

"Because you were angry and hurt when you left. Because I was angry and hurt that you were leaving. I didn't know how to make it okay after everything that had been said. You were better off without me."

"I've never been better off without you, Sam. If anything, I should have let you know that. I want to work on this. I want to be part of this family again. I want what Mom would have wanted, us three brothers together." He held out his hand to Sam. "Do you think that's possible?"

"I hope so." Sam took his hand and jerked him into a quick one-armed hug.

"I'll try to come back soon." This time Brady meant it. He would schedule it months in advance if he had to, but he would make sure that he had time to visit Tawnee Valley. He had one last stop before leaving town. One last chance to convince Maggie to come with him.

Chapter Twenty-One

Brady knocked on Maggie's door. He wanted to talk to Maggie alone.

The door opened and there she was. His mood lightened at the sight of her.

"Amber's not due home for another thirty minutes from Penny's." Maggie had that stubborn tilt to her jaw, but now it made him want to smile. "If you are here for the internet—"

He stepped closer and kissed her. Her hands went to his shoulders as if she was going to push him away, but instead he felt her fingers grip tight to his shirt. He could spend days kissing Maggie and never get his fill. Thirty minutes suddenly didn't seem like enough time.

Gently he guided her into the house with his body, because he was damned if he was going to stop kissing her if this was all he was going to get for a while. He closed the door with a kick. Like a starved man presented with food, he couldn't help himself when it came to Maggie. She filled a need he hadn't realized he had.

Her tongue lightly stroked his. Heat surged in his system. No other woman had this effect on him. Scary as it was, he didn't want to leave her behind. If that took marrying her, he would do it. Whatever she needed to feel comfortable.

He lifted his lips from hers and touched her forehead with his. Their heavy breaths mingled in the small entryway. She clung to his shirt. He held her like a desperate man, hoping to never let go.

"Reconsider, Maggie." He wanted to beg, to grovel, to worship her until she couldn't think straight.

Her hazel eyes met his. The green sparkled in the light while the brown around her pupils pulled him into their depths. A touch of wistfulness filled her eyes. Her smile tugged at the little piece of hope he had left.

"You are persistent."

"When I want something? Yes." He didn't step back. Wanted her to remember what it felt like to be with him. She said she loved him, but he was reluctant to use that as a bargaining chip.

"Why don't we go inside and talk this through? We should be able to find a manageable solution." Maggie pressed lightly against his shoulders.

He released her for the moment. *"Manageable solution?"*

She shrugged and took a seat at the dining room table, patting the chair next to her.

Time was against him in this negotiation. Maybe he should pull out all his big cards right away. He took the seat.

"I know you want us to move with you to New York." She held up her hand to stop him from talking. "This town is the only home Amber and I have ever known. You aren't asking us to move across the town but to another dimension."

He raised his eyebrow. *"Dimension?"*

"I've been there. I've seen all those people so driven to get to the next spot that they are as likely to mow you down as go around you. That style might suit you, Brady. But it's not who Amber and I are." She folded her hands together on the table. "It's not who I want Amber to become."

"You would get used to it. We would be together. Isn't that what family is about?" A low blow, but time was running short.

"Family is about finding what is best for everyone," Maggie said softly.

"My being employed—isn't that what's best?" Brady stood. Energy bounced through his body, making it impossible to sit still. He paced the carpeted floor. "What I do for a living isn't something I can do anywhere. I have to be in New York to be effective at my job. We don't have to live in Manhattan. We could move to a suburb."

"It's not just the city. You are asking us to give up what we have here. You aren't the only one who works. The furniture store lets me work flexible hours with Amber's schedule. I have friends who love me. A community that looks out for us. You can't offer that to us." Maggie remained surprisingly calm.

Didn't she realize what this meant? Didn't she realize his plans now included her? What would make her change her mind? "Isn't that what family is for? Isn't that what love is about?"

Her expression clouded over as she stood. "You have no right to tell me about love."

"Show me. Teach me what I need to know." Brady didn't want to leave like this. He wanted her to come with him.

She shook her head and backed away. "I can't."

"Why not?"

"Because it isn't something you learn." She hugged herself and leaned against the wall. "I wish I could help you, but you have to find it on your own."

Brady moved in front of her and caressed her cheek. "Maggie, I have to leave. Today. I don't want to go until I have your promise that you will consider the possibility of moving. Of making our family whole."

"More promises?" Her eyes filled with tears. "What about your promise of time?"

"It's unavoidable. My career is hanging on this project. I have to fix it." Brady dropped his hand. A few days away from work and the whole project depended on one meeting. He couldn't lose everything. He had to keep his career.

"Your career." Her voice was flat, emotionless. But her eyes were a deeper shade of green than he'd ever seen them.

"What's that supposed to mean?" he said.

She shook her head. That hated pity came into her eyes. "When you figure it out, let me know."

The door opened behind them.

"Daddy!" Amber tackle-hugged him from behind. "I'm glad you're here."

Maggie slipped away from him, but he couldn't wash her image from his mind. Why couldn't she understand?

Amber let go and rummaged through her backpack. He had to resolve this thing with Maggie. Amber deserved to have a family.

"How was school?" he asked. Maggie had disappeared, maybe to give him time to say goodbye to Amber or maybe to clear the tears. Eventually, she'd give in and come to him. He needed to give her more time to adjust to the idea.

"It was awesome." Amber held out a piece of red paper. "We are having an art show this Thursday. Can we make this our special outing?"

Her eyes sparkled with hope and love. He loved Amber. It was natural. But he couldn't reconcile what he felt for Maggie. Right now, the fact that he had to cancel Amber and his outing ripped his heart in two.

"I'm sorry, Amber." He wished he didn't have to ever say those words to her again. "I have to go to New York today."

Her smile turned into a frown. "But you'll be back."

Needing to be eye to eye, he got on one knee in front of her. "It's not that simple. I need to go back to work, but as soon as I get time off, I'll be back."

She sniffled and her lower lip trembled. He felt like the world's biggest jerk.

"It's okay, Daddy." She put her arms around his neck. "I'll miss you."

That made him feel even lower, but he wrapped his arms around her tight. "I'll miss you, too."

She pulled away and smooshed his face in her hands. She placed a single kiss on his forehead. When she pulled away, he smiled at her.

"What was that for?"

"Nana says that when you love someone and they are going to leave you, you should kiss their forehead to seal you into their memory. Nana always kissed me right here before I went to sleep." She pointed to a spot on her forehead.

"Your nana was a wise woman. I bet you miss her."

Amber nodded. "But she's right up here whenever I miss her too much."

"Would it be okay if I kissed your forehead, too? That way you don't forget about your daddy?" Tears welled in the back of Brady's throat as she nodded yes and leaned her forehead forward.

He kissed her lightly next to the spot her nana always kissed her. "I'll get back as soon as I can. I promise."

"I'll wait for you." Amber grabbed her bag and ran into the kitchen.

Brady stood slowly. This house was home to two people he cared so much about. If only he could box it up and take it with him. Including the wobbly kitchen chair and the recliner it took a good shove to recline in. It was as unique as Maggie and Amber.

A movement by the kitchen doorway pulled his attention. Maggie stood there. Her blond hair in a ponytail. Her hazel eyes watchful. Her lips slightly curved in a sad smile.

He wanted to stay, but he had to go. Within two strides, he had her in his arms. Maybe he couldn't convince her to go with him this time, but he'd keep trying. He kissed her lightly on her mouth before touching his lips to her forehead.

"Don't forget me, Maggie."

Back in New York that night, Brady stood alone in his apartment. Since he was early, no flowers warmed every room. However, the guest bedroom had begun its transformation. A soft lavender covered the walls and the old furniture was gone. Painter drop cloths were placed on the floor to protect the wood.

It remained an empty shell. Brady sighed and went to his bedroom to unpack. Maggie's red silk scarf called to him. He dropped to the bed and pulled the silk into his hands. Though it seemed like the only living thing in the apartment, it wasn't truly alive. That spark had come from Maggie.

His phone rang, breaking the silence.

"I'll get the files from my backup drive," Brady told Jules.

"I could have handled the meeting on my own."

Maybe she could, maybe she couldn't, but the fact of the matter was Brady had returned for just this purpose. To save his career and the job that consumed all his time.

"What time?"

"Nine." Jules paused. "Are you okay, Brady?"

His sanitized white room stared back at him. The emptiness of his apartment mocked him. No Maggie. No Amber. Just him.

"Yeah. I'll be fine. See you then." He disconnected the

call. When he went to work in the morning, he'd fall into his routine and have barely any time to think about what he'd left behind in Tawnee Valley.

He downloaded the files from his home server for the meeting tomorrow. Reviewed his notes and what Jules had emailed him. Everything was ready for tomorrow's meeting.

His apartment was empty. His life was empty. As he looked around, he wished he were in Tawnee Valley. Even the prospect of fighting for his project didn't thrill him. He couldn't imagine being here without Maggie and Amber. In a little over a week, they'd come to mean everything to him. But all he had left was his career. Maggie had made it clear that she did not want to move to New York.

Unfortunately, he couldn't get Maggie out of his head as he lay in bed, trying for sleep. He'd offered marriage, but she'd turned him down. Because she loved him. His chest filled with warmth. He hadn't had time to process her words before. Maggie Brown loved him. The sacrifices she made for her mother had been out of love. The sacrifices Sam had made had been out of love. And he'd expected her to follow him, sacrifice the life she'd built for herself and their daughter, because he wanted her with him. While he sacrificed nothing.

Brady pulled the red silk scarf through his fingers. How much more should everyone else sacrifice for him?

By the time exhaustion claimed him, his alarm clock went off. Even as tired as he was, Brady almost wished he had chores to do. Feeding the animals usually helped clear his head.

Instead, he rode the subway to his office and grabbed a coffee from the shop in the lobby. He needed a few days to settle back into his normal routine. Everything would return to normal.

Paperwork had piled up on his desk from last week. When

his meeting alert went off, Brady was feeling mostly human. The coffee and the monotony of paperwork had helped.

Jules came around the corner as he left his office. Her dark green suit was the top-of-the-line businesswear, but it didn't do anything for him. All he could think of were Maggie's bare feet on the runner board of her bed.

"I'm glad I caught up with you before the meeting," Jules said as they walked together toward Kyle's office.

"I've recovered all the files. We should be able to reassure Kyle that the project isn't leaking funds." Brady kept pace, but couldn't help remembering the slower walks with Amber and Maggie. Crisp autumn air and light conversation. Amber's giggles ringing through the streets.

"I had a chance to look through the preliminary numbers for the Tawnee Valley project you sent me," Jules said. "I think you might have something there. With a few tweaks, I bet we can get Kyle on board with the project."

"That sounds good." Brady paused outside Kyle's door. He placed a hand on Jules's sleeve to stop her from going in. "Do you think it's possible to love someone and not know it?"

Her forehead wrinkled as her perfectly arched eyebrows pulled toward each other. "What do you mean?"

"Sorry. Just preoccupied." Brady stepped aside for Jules to lead the way into Kyle's office.

"Have a seat," Kyle said.

The last time Brady had been in here he'd been focused on finding a way to make the project work and finding time to meet his daughter. On the far wall were portraits Brady hadn't noticed before. They showed various poses and ages of Kyle with his wife and their two children. Staged photos meant to show a happy family.

Very few of the family photos in Maggie's house had been staged with studio lighting.

"How did your visit with your family go, Brady?" Kyle regarded him with a piercing gaze.

"It went well. Very well." Except for the part where Maggie didn't want to live with him.

"Good. Jules, you had some problems to discuss." Kyle leaned back in his chair.

"We were able to recover the files for the budget. I think you'll be pleased with the calculations we've done. We're scheduled to come in right on budget with the Detrex project." Jules was all business, from her hair to her outfit to the way she carried herself. She had been everything Brady had thought he wanted.

"Peterson called to try to reschedule his meeting for this morning. Do you know anything about this?" Kyle looked at Brady first, but Brady turned to Jules.

"Given that Mr. Peterson grabbed my ass yesterday and suggested that the project would be back on track if I went out with him, my guess is he wanted to turn himself in on sexual harassment charges." Her cool demeanor didn't change.

"Why didn't you tell me this happened?" Brady could have done something about it.

Jules turned her cool gaze to him. "I don't need a protector, Brady. I can handle myself fine."

She'd said that before, but all of Brady's life he'd been taught to protect women. Now it seemed as if none of the women in his life needed him. Not Jules. Not Maggie.

"Those are some strong accusations. We take sexual harassment seriously in this organization. Would you be willing to report this in an incident report?" Kyle kept his gaze on Jules.

"Of course."

"Do you mind if I call in Mr. Peterson?"

Jules crossed her arms. A smug little smile formed on her lips. "No, sir. I don't mind at all."

Within minutes, Peterson stood in the room as far away from Jules as possible. Both Brady and Kyle stared at the bruise on the man's cheekbone. Brady resisted the urge to smile.

"Suspension without pay pending litigation." Kyle didn't seem unhappy to watch security escort Peterson grumbling from his office. When the door closed, Kyle addressed Jules, "It doesn't have to go that far before we step in, Jules."

She nodded. All this time, Brady had thought he was protecting her, but she could handle it on her own. Just like Maggie. It wouldn't matter if Detrex succeeded because Maggie wouldn't be there. If he wanted his family, maybe it was time to stop asking them to sacrifice for him and instead make some sacrifices of his own.

"I want off the Detrex project."

Surprised, Jules and Kyle faced him.

"Jules doesn't need my help. She can handle the account and take the project where it needs to be."

Jules flushed, but didn't say anything. Kyle nodded his agreement, but Brady wasn't finished yet.

"I want to talk to you about another project, though. If you have time," Brady said.

"My ten o'clock just got escorted from the building. What were you thinking?"

Chapter Twenty-Two

"And Jessica said pineapples come from special pine trees."
Amber walked backward to face Maggie. Obviously looking
for confirmation.

"I'm pretty sure this time Jessica is wrong." Maggie made
a circle motion with her finger to get Amber to face front and
watch where she was going.

"Daddy called yesterday."

Maggie stumbled but caught herself. "Did he?"

"Yup."

It had been almost a week since he'd left. The only other
time he'd called she'd been outside. Amber had been hanging up the phone as Maggie walked in. Maybe it was better
this way. Cut off all contact with him.

"He misses us." Amber spun in a circle. They were walking home from her Girl Scout meeting.

"Does he?" Maggie highly doubted that. He was probably
too wrapped in whatever his next project was to even make
time to think about them.

"Yeah, and he hopes to see us real soon." Amber took off running for the house.

Maggie hoped that Brady meant it. Not for her sake but for Amber's. Amber would get her hopes up and when Brady failed to meet her expectations, it would be Maggie's responsibility to soothe the hurt. Maggie's own father had contacted her two times after he left. Both times he'd promised to stop by next time he was in town. She'd sat outside and waited until she fell asleep on the porch swing.

Amber shouldn't have to go through that.

Penny had convinced Sam to watch Amber Friday night. Penny was determined to take Maggie out drinking and to find someone to take the edge off, as Penny put it.

A small part of Maggie held out hope that Brady would come to his senses, but even if he did, she wasn't sure she could trust it. What would he be willing to say to be able to have Amber in New York? After all, he'd already proposed marriage.

"Mommy, hurry." Amber's voice sounded far away.

Maggie searched the sidewalk, but she was only a few houses away from their house. Amber must have run ahead and let herself in.

As Maggie reached their sidewalk, she happened to look on the porch. Sitting on the top step holding a bouquet of fresh-picked wildflowers was Brady Ward. She stopped as her breath caught and her heart skipped a beat.

In jeans and a gray T-shirt, he sat on her porch, looking at her. Her mind couldn't process anything.

When he walked her way, she noticed movement in the screen door behind him. Penny and Amber smiled before they ducked away.

"I picked these for you." Brady held out the bouquet. A jumbled mess of goldenrod, black-eyed Susans and a blue flower she couldn't remember the name of. They were the most beautiful flowers she'd ever received. She took the bouquet warily. If he started in on New York again… She had to stay strong.

"I realized something while I was away."

She wasn't sure she was strong enough to meet his gaze. This was the man she loved, but it didn't take a degree to realize he wasn't going to love her in return.

"What did you realize?" Maggie took a deep breath filled with the scent of wildflowers.

"I've been searching for something my whole life. In high school, I thought if I was number one all the time that I would feel like part of this town. When I went to England, I thought if I rose to the top of the corporate ladder, I would feel like part of the company. When I moved to New York, I thought maybe this time it would be different."

When he didn't continue, she finally lifted her gaze to his. Her heart beat out of control. This was the one man who could get under her skin and stay there even though he was hundreds of miles away. How many times could she tell him no? How many times would her heart break over Brady Ward?

"When you came to me in New York, I thought maybe this was it. All I had to do was be an awesome dad and I would fill this hole in me." He reached out and brushed a strand of hair from her face.

"Did it?" Maggie was terrified to hear his answer but if she was ever going to be free to find love, she had to.

"Maggie, I didn't need to leave this town to find what I needed most in life. I got a little screwed up along the way, but when you walked back into my life, you gave me clarity again. You gave me a daughter. You gave me your love. Without wanting anything in return."

She held her breath. But she did want something in return. She wanted his love more than she wanted her next breath.

"I suck at this without PowerPoint." He smiled as he closed the distance between them, without touching her.

"I can't." Tears welled in her eyes. "I can't move to New York. If I thought it was the best thing for Amber, I would do it in a heartbeat, but I would die every day, knowing you don't love me."

His thumb caught her tear. "See, I'm making a mess of this. Amber told me the other day about how much fun she had with her friends. How they'd spent the afternoon picking flowers. I can't imagine taking that away from her. Or from you."

Maggie drew in a breath of air, aware of the press of her chest against his. "Then why are you here?"

He took her hands. "Because this is where I belong, Maggie. You are where I belong. All this time I thought I needed to be number one, but the only one I need to be number one for is you, Maggie Brown."

"What?" Tears raced down her cheeks, even as her heart lifted in her chest.

"I thought that by you moving to New York I would have everything, but I would have fallen into the same patterns. Work too much and not stop to really listen to you and Amber. My whole world there centered on work and getting to the next level."

"What are you trying to say?"

"You sacrificed your college for your mother and Amber. Sam took care of Luke and almost sacrificed the farm to help you out. I've done nothing to prove to you that I love you and want to be with you." He took her hands in his.

Her heart raced. "How do you know you love me and not just the idea of a family?"

He smiled and pressed a quick kiss to her lips. "I've been a fool. Afraid to love, afraid to have a family need me. You are the one who soothed me when things felt out of control.

You are the one who gave me strength when I needed it. Before Amber was even in the picture, I needed you. Even before I knew the real Maggie Brown. Something about you has always drawn me.

"I love you with all my heart. I want us to be a family. I don't need New York as long as I have you and Amber. I want to show you how much I love you for the rest of my life. Right here in Tawnee Valley. My company is starting a new project and I've asked to take lead. We're building a factory here. If I have to stay at Sam's and come to your house every day to ask you if you'll marry me, I will."

Tears welled in her eyes and choked her throat. Never in her life had she imagined he would love her.

"I hope those are tears of happiness. I love you, Maggie Brown. I want to marry you. If I have to beg, I will." He started to drop to his knee, but she caught his elbow.

She drew in a deep breath and blinked rapidly to help the tears go away. "All I ever wanted was your love. If I thought you loved me, I would have moved to New York in a heartbeat."

"Now you don't have to." He kissed her. "Say you'll marry me, Maggie. That we'll live here in Tawnee Valley and grow old together."

Looking into his beautiful blue eyes, Maggie knew she was lost and found at the same time. "Yes, I'll marry you."

Her heart felt as if it was going to burst from happiness as he gathered her in his arms.

* * * * *

HARLEQUIN®

SPECIAL EDITION

Life, Love and Family

Be sure to check out the last book in this year's
THE FORTUNES OF TEXAS:
SOUTHERN INVASION
miniseries by Crystal Green.

Free-spirited Sawyer and fiercely independent
Laurel seem like two peas in a pod. But their
determination to keep things casual backfires when
Mr. I Don't suddenly decides he wants a bride!

Look for *A CHANGE OF FORTUNE* next month
from Harlequin® Special Edition®.
Available wherever books and ebooks are sold!